Echoed Heartbeats

When you feel his heart beat next to yours

A Collection of Love Stories
by

Linda Boulanger

Echoed Heartbeats
By Linda Boulanger

©2013 Linda Boulanger

Cover Design/Interior Design
www.TellTaleBookCovers.weebly.com

Published by TreasureLine Publishing
www.TreasureLinePublishing.weebly.com

ISBN: 978-1-61752-162-1

PRINTED IN THE UNITED STATES OF AMERICA

For those of you who have
found what you're looking for,
and for those still waiting...

Believe

Alone. A place I would rather not be. Yet, here I am. No one but me. I bow my head, afraid. Where are you? Where did *we* go?

Tears flow into my hands, through my fingers. I watch them pool on the ground at my feet. And then I see ... a reflection. Alone is a place I will never be. No matter what, I will always have me.

In This Collection:

Up to Bat

Tiny eyes watched him as they moved away. The baby stared, unassuming, not caring about anything beyond the comfort received from being draped over a familiar shoulder. Darvis smiled, laughed at himself for even questioning whether the baby could have been his. When his eyes locked with Cari's and his brows raised, she'd shaken her head and laughed. My sister's baby, she'd mouthed as if he should have known. Hell, he'd never been around pregnant women or babies before. He'd never thought about the timing or how it all worked other than how they were made. Three and a half months ago he'd spent a night in heaven with his lips pressed against the same shoulder the baby mouthed in contentment. He'd been pretty content with the sweet taste of the woman that owned it, too. Yep, with all they'd done, he was pretty sure they could have easily made a baby.

Instead, she'd just up and walked away.

The elation he felt at seeing her again vanished, replaced by a resurgence of the ache that had wrapped itself around his heart when he'd realized she was gone. Just like that. In his arms one minute, promising to meet him after the game the next, and then, before his bat was even back in his bag, she was gone. No note. No call. Just … gone.

Ben Darvis sighed as he looked down at his cleated feet where he stood in the hallway beneath the stadium. He could hear his teammates in the locker room just down the way, a few of them had ventured into the weight room, and a couple more had managed to persuade one of the young trainers to offer up a round on the massage tables.

"Good to finally know why she left in such a hurry, huh?"

Darvis swung around coming face-to-face with the team's publicity manager. An older woman, in her late forties maybe, Angela Carrigan was the poster child for kindness, though there wasn't a guy on the team that didn't respect her and her ability to get things done. She'd almost single-handedly put the team back on the map, doing more for their reputation and their zeal by getting them multi-million dollar endorsements, working with the likes of T.D. Barruda and other big time sports product manufacturers to provide high dollar outfits and equipment just so they could say the now-winning Commanders used their stuff.

Angela Carrigan had also been the one to bring Carissa on board, hiring her in an unusual publicity move to do pencil sketch drawings of the players during the games. The images were then broadcast over the huge screens at the ends of the field off and on through the games as well as placed here and there in the programs sold at the next game. Ben had to admit, he'd thought it was a stupid idea at first, but the fans seemed to eat it up. There was even a calendar in the works, using actual photos of the players paired with Carissa's pencil drawings as the backgrounds, which was the reason she'd been on the road with them in the first place –to get the rest of her drawings. The young artist had been sorely missed by the fans and the players alike after her sudden departure. Some players more than others, obviously.

Angela cleared her throat causing Ben to jump. She smiled when he looked up. Her eyes told him she knew more than anyone that the budding friendship between him and the coach's niece had progressed beyond amiable companionship.

"Uhm. Yeah. It's too bad about her sister getting *sick* right at the time the baby was born." He stumbled, mumbled, trying to find words. "Nice of Cari to step in."

"She couldn't tell anyone, you know. Not that she *couldn't*. More that … well, you know people always think the mental health of family members will reflect badly on them. And with her sister being her twin and all…"

Angela's words hung there with Darvis trying to comprehend what she was actually telling him.

"Her leaving wasn't meant to hurt you, even though it did. She simply knew her sister needed her and everything else took a back seat." She waited for him to digest what she'd said. "She looked tired and more than a little bit stressed to me. I'm thinking she could use a friend now that she's decided it's time to resurface. And I'd say from the look in her eyes, she wouldn't mind too much if that someone was you."

Darvis' innards filled with hope right before his heart plummeted into a doubtful spiral, all in a matter of seconds. "I don't know, Ang. She's known all along where to find me. She knew and didn't."

Angela shook her head and he knew she was wondering whether he'd heard a word she'd said. He had. Didn't keep his heart from hurting though. Or his pride. She should have at least called.

His mind roamed back to that night with Cari, the one and only time she'd gone on the road with them, the first time he'd admitted he had feelings for the spunky twenty-something with her sandy blond ponytail and ready smile. Just thinking about her turned up the corners of his mouth. It also caused a painful pinch right behind the wall of his finely sculpted chest, especially when he allowed himself to remember the way she'd traced those planes with soft fingertips before her lips had followed suit. She'd lifted her head and laughed, a soft melody, right before she'd declared that she'd never tire of waking up beside him.

And then she'd sobered, her forehead crinkling with a frown. He hadn't offered her forever, hadn't looked beyond that night. And she hadn't asked even as she'd given herself to him, the first man she'd ever been with. His chest constricted with the thought. What a fool he'd been.

"I'm sorry," she'd whispered trying to pull away, attempting to pull the covers between them.

Ben had pushed aside that little pinch, along with

the sheet. He'd resisted the right and wrong warring inside of him, instead kissing her neck, her shoulder, before whispering in return, "We have now…"

And they had. Right then, they'd made love again before the sunlight filtered in the reality of why they were there. Right before he'd left her to prepare to pitch his team to victory. Right before she'd walked away, without so much as a phone call to explain why.

"Ben." She'd stopped to look back at him.

She flinched when he lifted his eyes to hers. He knew she could see the anger flaring within their hazel depths. Her head dropped and she turned around. Ben focused on the barely visible little head now resting in the crook of her arm as she walked away. Another inward battle launched itself around his heart.

"Cari, wait."

She stopped, though only for a moment before she started walking again, calling back over her shoulder, "It's okay, Ben. I understood then, and I understand now. I just thought…" She shook her head.

"You thought what?" he asked, catching up to her, careful not to knock the tiny head when he grabbed her arm.

She looked up at him, her eyes searching his. He hoped she would see his plea. He needed her to say what he hoped she was trying to say, needed her to feel what he was feeling. He felt more nervous than he did whenever he stepped up to bat!

"I've really missed… I've missed the team." Her half laugh broke at the end, her eyes flitting around his face.

It was time to swallow his pride. "Just the team, Car? As a whole?"

She closed her eyes as he touched her cheek. She shook her head then looked at him again. "Some more than others."

With a trembling smile she turned her face into his hand and kissed his palm, making his knees go weak. Him! Some star ball player he was.

Careful not to crush the tiny life that had separated them months ago, he pulled her as close to him as he could. That separation had actually been the key. Without it he wondered if he would have realized what she truly meant to him, how much he wanted her to be a part of the rest of his life, how much he looked forward to them creating a new life. Had he not pretty much told her there may or may not be a *them*. Instead, she'd gone and he'd had time to think. Lots of lonely minutes filled with thoughts of her. His arms tightened around her, pulling her closer to him.

"Sorry, little guy." He laughed when the baby stretched and knocked against him seeming to push him away. He looked back at Cari. "I'm afraid I don't know much about these little people."

"But you're okay with babies? You, uh, you want kids of your own?"

Ben's brows drew down. She looked awfully hopeful for someone who was unsure of where they'd been headed that she'd walked away. "Uhm. Yeah. I just …"

"Ben," she cut him off, a finger pressed to his lips.

She took a deep breath, letting it out in a huff of nervousness. "Part of the reason I came down here... I needed to see you... I needed to tell you... That night..."

Ben's own nervousness spiked, not because of what he thought she might be trying to say but because of her delivery. "That night was heaven, Cari. And I was a fool to have let you walk away. But it's okay. We'll be okay. Just tell me what it is you have to say." His hands where gentle on her shoulders, the baby seemed to still as he too waited. Ben saw only Cari, his eyes now held the hope hers had. He urged her to continue with a nod of his head.

She smiled then bit at her lower lip. "I'm glad you want kids, Ben. Because I came down here to find you... I wanted to tell you in person that in about five and a half months you'll be up to bat."

Center Stage

Blue. It was the only way to describe the way Jenna Evans was feeling. Descending on her the moment she'd laid eyes on Pierce Colton that evening, the feeling began at the top of her head and drained down like a thick, encompassing liquid flowing over her entire body.

She knew she'd better master control over this feeling and needed to do it fast. In just moments the emcee would announce her name, fans would start cheering, and she'd be expected to meet Pierce Colton center stage with a smile on her face and her lips ready to collide with his for a show starting kiss that girls around the world would kill for.

And yet misery coated her insides.

"I hate you. I hate you. I hate you." She wondered how many times she would have to say those words for her heart to believe them. Throughout her usual pre-show ritual -- rolling her neck, shaking her arms, shifting her weight from foot-to-foot – she could see Pierce across the stage. He was chatting quietly, probably with some woman. Her hate-o-meter rose another degree and she intensified the ritualistic movements. Pierce Colton was not going to derail her career by turning her insides to jelly and her mind to mush simply because he'd pushed her away right after she'd given him her heart. Well, he may not want her in his personal life, but he had no choice but to keep her around as his business partner, at least until this concert tour was over.

She had to admit, teaming up with the top male country artist had given her career the boost it desperately needed. Unlike the majority of those in the music industry, Jenna hadn't ridden in on the coattails of a famous mother or an uncle in the business. She hadn't slept her way to the top either. No, she'd worked hard to get where she was. And that place was at the top since she'd teamed up with Pierce.

She remembered back to how skeptical she'd been when the proposal of a tour with him had been suggested. But the chemistry between them exploded the first time they met. And the rest, as they say, was history in the making. With Pierce Colton beside her, Jenna Evans, known to the world as Jenna Roxanne, had finally *arrived*, positioned on the horizon of superstardom.

Working with Pierce, up until now, had been amazing. He'd pushed her beyond her comfort zone, demanding more from her as an artist than she'd ever thought possible. He'd even taken her shopping to *spice up* her wardrobe. He'd molded her into the woman the public would clamor to see.

"The world's yours for the taking, doll," he'd told her right before he'd suggested the shopping trip. Spoken with that sexy country accent of his, he'd continued, "But, you have to learn how to work it.

You're a beautiful woman, Jenna Roxanne." He'd trailed a finger from temple to jawline, then down her neck to outline the matronly cut of her shirt's collar. "They want to see what you have to offer…"

He'd stared down at her as his words faded, his eyes dropping to her lips just long enough that she'd thought for sure he was going to kiss her. Instead he'd tapped her on the nose in big brother fashion and suggested he take her shopping. Stunned, Jenna could do little more than nod and away they'd gone.

Jenna sighed. If she was honest with herself, she'd have to admit that was when her heart started slipping into his grasp, though it had taken several months of writing, recording, rehearsing, and finally being on the road together for him to make his move and for her to let him. What a fool, she thought, allowing herself a moment more to wallow in the thick syrup of misery before returning her focus to the stage before her. She knew the spiel, knew the emcee was getting ready to announce them, knew it was time to put on her game face and let the people have what they'd paid for. Broken heart or no, Jenna Roxanna was all about being professional.

"…And now, the moment you've all been waiting for. Give it up for Piercccccce Colton and Jennnna Roxxxxxxannnne…."

The crowd erupted as the duo entered their view from opposing sides of the stage. Pierce had the audacity to look her over then wink as she came toward him. Undoubtedly he recognized the outfit. He'd picked it out. Jenna reached for his outstretched hand, their fingertips barely touching before he grabbed hold of her, pulled her tight against his broad chest, and spun her around. Through a fog, Jenna heard the roaring crowd, heard their chant. *Kiss her, kiss her, kiss her*!

Her body firmly against his, unwanted desire flare as Jenna remembered how it had felt to be in his arms, wrapped in a lover's embrace that had carried them through the night. What was worse, she knew Pierce felt it too. With a deliberate slowness, he slid her back down his body to where her feet were planted firmly on the stage.

"I missed you this morning," he whispered as his fingers snaked back into her hair. "Thought you were going to join me for breakfast?"

Jenna frowned and his brows drew down before one lifted in question.

"If I didn't know better, I'd say you've been trying to avoid me all day, doll."

KISS HER!!!

Pierce left her no time to respond. He smiled that so-sexy-it-makes-your-insides-tremble   trademark smile of his, turning his head toward the audience for a brief moment before he closed the gap and his mouth covered Jenna's. Only unlike every other night, the kiss deepened, his tongue tracing the curve of her lips before requesting entrance. Jenna's mouth seemed to have a mind of its own, opening to allow him inside just as it had, over and over, throughout the night.

"It aaaaall started… with a kisssssss…" Pierce started the song, turning away from a dazed Jenna to face the expectant audience. He continued, crooning about that first kiss and how she'd worked her way into his heart.

Jenna managed to snap out of it just in time to belt out her part, answering back in the style so typical of country duets. The audience always ate it up though, especially after that shared kiss.

Somehow Jenna managed to get through the show. After the final bows, she slipped into the wings. Pierce's behavior and questions had left her with more than a few questions of her own and she needed to be alone to think.

"Jenna?"

Busted. Jenna froze on her way down the stairs to the limo that would have returned her to their hotel. The disappointment in Pierce's voice had stopped her feet more than anything.

"What's going on, doll?"

Jenna's head dropped. It took her several minutes and the fear of Pierce moving closer to help her find her voice. "I came down to the hotel restaurant, just like you'd asked when you slipped away from my room. Only..." Jenna cleared her emotion-clogged throat. "You weren't alone, Pierce." Her eyes filled with tears that refused to stay put. One slid down her cheek and brought him exactly where she didn't want him: to her side.

A gentle thumb wiped the tear away, his palm remaining against her cheek. "Will you come with me for a minute?"

Jenna shook her head, shook his hand away. "No,

I just need to go."

It was no use. He already had her hand and was pulling her back up the stairs. Jenna walked with her head down not wanting anyone to see the remaining moisture on her cheeks.

"Krissy!"

Jenna's head popped up at the sound of Pierce's voice, her mouth dropped open as they approached the very woman he'd been with that morning at breakfast. Jenna started trying to backpedal, to get him to release her. Pierce seemed oblivious, hauling her to a stop in front of the gorgeous blond.

"Jenna Evans, I want you to meet someone who is more special to me than just about anyone on this earth. This is Krissy. Krissy Colton, my sister."

The blonde held out her hand, which Jenna just stared at. More special... His... What?

"I'm assuming by your reaction you didn't know I was coming. Seems Pierce may have had something else on his mind that caused my arrival to be forgotten. Good thing I knew the hotel and bumped into him at breakfast." She laughed. It was Pierce's melodic laugh in a feminine dose.

"I'm sorry. I'm just..." Jenna fumbled, finally settling on a smile and an outstretched hand. "It's very nice to meet you."

"Krissy's been a fan of yours for years, doll. In fact, it was her prodding that got me to agree to meet you in the first place." Pierce nodded as Jenna looked from sister to brother.

"And I'm hoping Pierce's request for me to bring

Grandma's ring means what I think it means." Krissy smiled.

Jenna felt numb in a good sort of way, only she seemed unable to breathe. Pierce took her hand and pulled her to him very much like he did every night at the start of the show.

"It all started long before that first kiss for me, Jenna, and I've been trying to figure out a way to let you know. And, just in case, I had Krissy bring me the ring." He brushed his lips over hers before continuing. "Having to leave your side after last night … I don't think I can do that again. So what I'm trying to say is that I'd be honored if you'd consider sharing center stage with me for the rest of our lives."

Fresh tears filled her eyes as she stared up at him, knowing center stage with Pierce Colton was exactly where she was supposed to be. Jenna Roxanne had definitely arrived.

Best Friend Rules

I brushed my hands over the skirt of my new sundress before sitting down at one of those charming little tables outside a beachfront bar type place. It was the cutest dress, sent to me by the man I was waiting to meet - my bestest friend in the whole world, Jack Jackman. Weird name. And not his real first name, of course. I mean, who names their kid practically the same name first and last? That would be like my parents naming me Samantha Samson or something like that. You just don't do that. Though it sounded kind of cute, actually.

"Sammi Samson." I tried it out. Huh. I kind of liked it. Only my last name was Jones. You know, as in keeping up with the... I rolled my eyes. My parents, well, my mother to be more exact, was definitely into keeping up with and going beyond others. Let me tell you...

No, let me don't. This isn't a story about my mom so don't even get me started! Let's head back to Brock instead.

Brock? Oh, right! Well, you see, Brock is Jack's real name. Only he hates it with a passion. I think it was one of those names passed down from generation to generation and he got stuck with it, being the first born male in his family. Poor guy. It probably didn't help any that I teased him without mercy about that name when we were kids. I know! To do that broke all the best friend rules, but it was just too good to be true, getting thrown together in life with a guy whose first name is Brock … rhymes with Bok – you know, the sound a chicken makes as it struts around? Huh. Maybe only roosters strut. I don't know. But I do know I was not a good friend about that name and Brock somehow managed to get everyone, even his own parents, to call him Jack before we reached Jr. High.

Everyone except *my* mother. I rolled my eyes, thankful they came out of that spiral motion to lock on the lovely distraction before me. Four very delicious looking guys playing sand volleyball right there on the beach in front of me.

And that's when it happened. As I took a slow sip of my delectably fruity drink in the tall glass with the short stem, with just the right amount of liquid courage added in, their ball came whizzing past my head to plop with a thump on the sand behind me. I turned to look at it, then back around to see one of the four guys heading my way and I forgot all about my mother. I could not take my eyes off that delicious scoop of tan-drenched man headed straight toward me.

Well, maybe not *straight* toward me, but certainly in my direction. Yes, he was definitely checking out my new dress and looking at me. Me! I felt my insides start to slither around just like they always did when I encountered a cute guy that I knew would quickly realize what a dork I really was right before he made his escape. I glanced down to make sure there wasn't anything on the front of my shirt and prayed nothing was stuck between my teeth that would have drawn his attention instead of me. Then I looked back at him and tried to smile. It must have passed for some semblance of a friendly gesture because he spoke to me.

"Hi. How you doing?" His voice was as smooth and yummy as a desirable piece of absolutely-good-for-you-in-every-way dark chocolate.

I nodded, unable to speak since my lungs had forgotten breathing was necessary to sustain life. With a sputter, they restarted and I loudly sucked in a gulp of air in a most unladylike manner that resulted in a short, hand-over-mouth coughing fit. See. You're a dork, I thought before melting into my chair to direct myself with a whispered chant.

"Breathe, breathe, breathe."

It should have made me feel better, and probably would have, if it hadn't been for the sound of masculine chuckling drifting over my right shoulder.

The site that met me when I wheeled around did not last nearly long enough. I came face-to... well, face-to-scrumptious derriere. But he straightened up too quickly from where he'd bent to retrieve the ball. Man, I should have turned around earlier. Earth to Samantha! I pulled my eyes back up from the ball now clutched against his superbly short shorts clad hip, not missing a single inch of those abs and that chest, toned to perfection. And that perfectly chiseled jaw, scrumptiously full lips lifted at the corners, only slightly upturned nose crinkled with mirth…

Then it hit me. He'd only come this way because of the ball. He wasn't checking me or my sundress out at all. I'd done it again. Dork! I felt the heat rising up my neck and over my cheeks.

"You okay?" His eyes, a most peculiar shade of deep green, opened wide, his brows shot up toward the tousle of dark brown waves on top of his perfect head.

Seriously? Had he never seen anyone blush before? I gave him my best *what's-wrong-with-you?* glare, then jumped back, mortified, when he flung the ball away and dropped to his knees beside my chair and reached out a hand to touch my cheek.

"What the…" I'm sure my eyes were as big as his, though not nearly as beautiful. Hazel eyes weren't particularly beautiful, in my opinion, though I'd been told before that my eyes were one of my better features. I was never sure whether I should take that as an insult or compliment. Anyway… I really had been daydreaming that he'd fall for me somehow, but this was a bit unexpected and … disturbing in an odd sort of way.

"Raphe! I think you'd better bring the EpiPen. She's swelling up like a tomato over here!"

Who was Raphe and what was he talking about? His brows had now drawn down in a deep V, concern radiating from those to-die-for eyes that seemed to be roaming over my face, neck, and arms.

That's when I felt it – the intense itching that accompanied the burning. Uh oh! I looked down to find he was right. I was covered in hives that were quickly turning from plural to singular, as in one giant hive all over my body.

"Peanut allergies?" he asked, noticing the bowl of half-eaten nuts on my table.

I shook my head and tried to swallow. Having him this close was making my mouth dry. Or maybe it was the allergic reaction. Either way, it was getting hard to breathe.

"RAPHE!!!"

I think my shallow breathes were starting to scare him. Gosh he was cute when he was scared. Who was I kidding? He was cute even when he wasn't. Duh! I wondered briefly if he'd catch me if I fell. My eyes were getting droopy and my limbs felt so heavy.

"Bout time!"

It took some work but I managed to follow his glare to see the man at the receiving end. Ah! Raphe – presumed with the exchange of what had to be the requested EpiPen. So Raphe must be the owner of this beachfront establishment. Otherwise, he was an imposter who'd sold me my *owner's special*. He'd told me he made them with a secret ingredient no one would expect to find mixed with fruit but gave it just the zap it needed to make it…special. I hadn't cared. I'd just wanted a drink.

"Peanut allergy?" the also superbly toned and tanned Raphe asked.

"She says no," Super Yummy answered since I didn't feel the need. We'd already been over that, hadn't we?

Man I was tired! Speaking of men…the others from the volleyball game decided to venture up right as

I decided to scrunch down farther into my seat. I sure hoped my skirt on my cute little sundress wasn't inching up as I slid down, not that I overly cared at that point. I just knew my head was too heavy for my neck and I had to rest it somewhere. It was either the back of the blasted low-back chair or Mr. Tan, still kneeling beside me. The thought of resting my head on his shoulder did have certain appeal…

"What about fruit?"

What about fruit? I tried to look at the barkeeper dude to glare at him. Who, in her right mind, orders a fruity drink knowing she's allergic to fruit?! Logic definitely wasn't his strong suit. But my eyes were too heavy to muster the glare so I settled for a weak headshake instead. Those eyes were definitely staying closed. Except they did flutter when I felt the unexpected poke of the EpiPen.

"Ouch! You really should warn a girl before you go poking her with one of those, you know," I managed.

Hot-n-Yummy chuckled. "Sorry about that. We needed to get that in you, love."

I nodded and sighed. Yes, I literally and embarrassingly sighed. Mr. Scrumptious was rubbing the spot where he'd jabbed me, ever so gently rubbing his smooth, warm hand over my arm. It seemed so…intimate!

Out of nowhere – okay, out of my overly active imagination – I could see the two of us sitting on a beach, our children frolicking in the waves not too far away while he caressed my arm and whispered in my ear…

"Oh, that feels good." I hoped the words hadn't really come out in the near-purr my ears heard.

They had. I could tell by the chuckles of the continually growing crowd and the heat on my neck and cheeks intensified.

Okay, that was it. I was tired of being the center attraction. Only when I bolted upright too quickly, I wasn't prepared for my body to have turned completely to jelly, and I found myself in the arms of an always-quick-to-respond salacious delicacy. So I practically fell on him as I'd sat upright and his choices were to catch me or be plowed. Either way, I was now wrapped in his arm, our faces so close I could feel his breath on my burning cheek, smell the scent of his masculine shampoo, and his eyes were locked with mine. And I wasn't really breathing anymore.

Oh, this was going from bad to worse! In fact, I wasn't sure it could get much worse.

"Ryan! What the hell are you doing with my best girl?!"

Guess I was wrong.

"Jeez! What did you do to her?" He glared at Ryan then smiled at me. "Dress looks nice. I told you she'd wear it, Ry."

Jack dropped down on the sand beside us while I tried to untangle myself from … Ryan. It appeared the tan-drenched god had a name. And he was Jack's friend.

And there I was, smiling up at him like a love-sick dork.

"Hi, Sammi." He returned the gesture, "I'm Jack's roommate. I've heard so much about you."

Now he was outright laughing, probably due in part to the loud groan I'd made before letting my forehead drop against his chest.

"Don't worry, love. I find your antics quite entertaining. In fact, I'm looking forward to seeing a bit more of them firsthand, maybe over dinner and a movie?"

Seriously? Was this absolutely gorgeous chunk of man actually sort of flirting with *me*? I could feel my heart rate rise as I looked back up at him and his smile told me he was.

"And you're Jack's bestie here?" My brows drew down.

So did his as he nodded, undoubtedly wondering where I was going with this.

"Isn't there a rule against all this? You know? *Thou shalt not date your best friend's best friend* or something along those lines?"

He laughed. "I think it says you can't date your best friend's boyfriend." He glanced at Jack, then back down to me. "And I am definitely not Jack's boyfriend."

Jack. I wondered what he was thinking about all this. His ear-to-ear grin told me I should have known better than to worry where he was concerned. I relaxed and smiled.

"You dork! Of course I don't mind." In true Jack fashion, he'd practically read my thoughts. "Why do you think I had you come out here?"

"To entertain you with my dorkiness?"

My heart swelled with love for this friend of mine … at least I hoped it was love and not some effect of the drug or allergy. Jack had to be the best friend any girl could have ever imagined.

"Come on, let's get you out of here, tomato girl," he said, rising and offering me a hand. I missed Ryan's warm, practically naked body immediately, though his arm was about my shoulder as soon as we started walking, no doubt to steady me. I knew enough about him from conversations with Jack to know the tasty dish was a med student. Made sense of his actions earlier. I briefly wondered if his bedside manner was this good with all his patients, though my thoughts quickly jumped to the fact that doctors don't carry those mysterious little black bags anymore…

"My bag, Jack. Can you grab it?"

Jack nodded and helped himself to a gulp of my drink while he was at it, which was okay because I didn't want it anymore. It had left an odd aftertaste of…

"Cinnamon!" we both said at the same time.

"You just had to have a Raphe Special, didn't you? The only drink in the world mixed with fruit soaked in cinnamon, which is the only thing in the world you're allergic to in quantity." Jack shook his head. "Sammi J. That is so you." He looked at Ryan and shook his head again. "You want to rethink this, Ry? This is the way life is with her."

Okay, so maybe Jack wasn't such a great friend after all.

"But she's very entertaining. Never a dull moment with her around," he added

"Dull has never been my style."

"You always have liked a challenge."

Ryan nodded. I smiled over at Jack who reached for my hand and for a moment I was transported back to childhood days, walking along with my best friend, our eyes locked. And then Ryan pulled me into an all-out hug … to steady me as I tripped over the only rock on the entire beach.

I suddenly felt better than I ever had about being clumsy, accident-prone me, especially if it was going to put me in this yummy man's arms every time.

"Your last name's not Samson by any chance, is it?"

It couldn't hurt to ask.

Face of an Angel

She lay there watching the life drain from her body one red drop at a time. The blood oozing from her wrist pooled then slipped over the side of her arm. Drip. Drip. Like Grandma's leaky faucet that no one seemed able to fix and Grandma refused to replace. That old thing annoyed everyone – the faucet, not her grandmother.

A smile touched lips so dry she thought they might crack – kind of like her life. Heavy lids lowered and lifted only to close again. She forced them open, looking at the blood, fascinated, fixated wondering what she had done.

A single tear slipped from her eye. Drop. It rolled down her face. Grandma was right. She was always acting on her emotions. But when she'd found out about Brad's affair, she'd been so hurt, so angry. She'd told him goodbye without waiting for an explanation, and left. It was time to end it. It was time for him to pay, not only for this time, but for all the others as well.

Now… She realized her impulsiveness might very well spell the end her life. Oh, God! She'd only wanted him to see how upset she was, how much he'd hurt her. She stared at the red pool growing larger. The blood dripped faster with the increased pumping of her heart. She cried out again. Would anyone find her? Could anyone help her now?

Grandma. A grim picture filled her head at the thought of the authorities delivering the news of her death. That information might well kill the old woman. No. Grandma always told her she would not rest until she saw her granddaughter on the road to happiness. Was death the road she was to take?

Thought became more difficult as she lay there. She didn't know the answers anymore, wondered if she ever had.

"I don't want to die," she whispered. Staring into the distance, she saw nothing, though through the fog clouding her head, she heard something. She strained to listen.

Hope.

The faint sound of distant sirens grew louder. She smiled and closed her eyes. Perhaps today was not the day for her to die.

"It'll be okay, Grandma." Her own voice sounded unfamiliar to her, detached, hollow. She squeezed her eyes tighter. They burned. Her arm throbbed. She wished she could feel her legs.

Tired. She couldn't remember ever being so tired. With a sigh, she allowed herself to drift off. It was okay to sleep now. They were coming…

"Hey, sister. Can you hear me?"

Laken tried to open her eyes when he touched her face. "Mmmm." She wondered if her voice was audible beyond her own body.

"Good girl. I'm Mark. I'm going to take care of you." His voice was so soothing, reassuring.

It took an awful lot of effort to look up at him. She smiled, or tried, before her lids closed again. "The face of an angel," she mumbled.

Laughter sounded from somewhere beside her as well as from above. "Don't let those pretty blue eyes fool you," the other voice told her. A male voice. Were all angels men? She tried to turn her head to see the other one.

"Hold still until we make sure you're okay. They're bringing in the jaws of life to get you out of this tangled mess."

She tried to nod but the angel's hands were on her face again, holding here head in place.

"Kev's working on your arm. It might hurt a bit. He needs to wash away all that blood to see how bad the wound is. Pretty nasty cut you got there. Pretty bad wreck."

"Looks like a glass shard maybe," Kev's voice told them. "It just nicked the vein. Thank goodness or she'd have been a goner…"

"Shhh!" Mark's voice was filled with warning. "You're going to be just fine, sis."

Laken didn't try to answer, didn't share that her life was in too big of a mess for her to truly be okay. Something sharp pierced her arm. She flinched.

"Just a little cocktail to help slow the blood flow and a little extra to ease the pain, sis," Mark reassured her. Laken wasn't sure whether she should tell him there was no pain. She couldn't feel anything, though the option of telling him was quickly taken out of her control as warmth flooded her body, relaxing her. She sighed, making the Mark angel laugh. "Feels good, doesn't it?" he whispered, somewhere close to her ear. "We save that special treat for the select few."

Again, she tried to smile, reassured by his teasing. She wished she could ask him what was going on though other voices interrupted. He seemed confident and in control as her vitals were exchanged. A female voice told him her name was Laken, saying she'd found her purse in the wreckage. That same voice indicated there appeared to have been no one else in the vehicle upon impact, though the person in the other car – sounded like they had not fared so well.

"Grandma," Laken managed with great effort. Only Mark's continued closeness to her head allowed him to hear.

"Laken? Was your grandmother with you?" She heard concern in his voice, imagined his dark brows drawn over those dreamy blue eyes.

"No," she whispered.

Mark's loudly exhaled breath signaled his relief. "We'll get a hold of her, then. Don't worry. Let's just concentrate on getting you free."

That was the last thing Laken remembered before waking in the hospital. Her grandmother sat on one side of her bed, the angel a few feet away on the other.

"Welcome back, sweetheart." Her grandmother's smile was priceless.

Laken returned her hug as best as she could, feeling jabs of glorious pain shoot throughout her body. She could feel! Pain had never been so welcomed.

She turned her head to the side. "Hi." Relief eased some of the lines around the man's tired eyes when she spoke to him. "What are you doing here?"

The angel looked at her grandmother. Alarm flooded through Laken's battered body.

"What's wrong?"

"Laken, honey…" her grandmother began in that tone reserved for bad news. "There was another car. Brad was driving it…"

"He…didn't make it, did he?"

Both heads shook, both sets of eyes watched her closely.

"The authorities would like to talk to you because…well, it appears as if he tried to force you off the road." Mark looked almost apologetic for having to ask. "Do you know of any reason he would have done that?"

He touched the spot on her left hand where her wedding ring had been. There was no way he could have known she'd removed it, throwing it at Brad before she ran from the house. Laken closed her eyes against threatening tears.

"Hang in there, sis." His voice was right next to her ear. "Sometimes sad endings can lead to happy beginnings." He squeezed her hand.

Laken opened her eyes, looking up into the most beautiful blue eyes she'd ever seen, hopeful eyes in the face of an earthly angel.

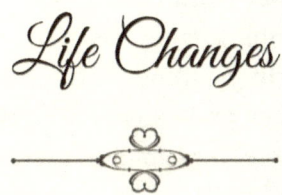

Life Changes

Chloe choked down a swallow of coffee and reached for the ringing phone.

"Hello!" Although the caller received her greeting, her eyes and attention remained on the computer screen before her. Who'd have thought organizing her artwork on her website would be such a difficult task? She certainly hadn't or she wouldn't have left it to the last minute. Tomorrow she had to forward the link for the new pages to a potential buyer in Paris. *Paris!* Chloe barely stifled a squeal at the thought that a Paris gallery wanted to see her artwork. If they chose to represent her, life would never be the same.

Her brain finally turned to the call, registering the silence on the other end. A deep crease etched into the porcelain expanse between her drawn eyebrows. "Hello? May I help you?" she asked attempting to keep felt concern from tainting her voice. Maybe it was the Paris gallery with a bad connection. She waited a couple more seconds before continuing. "Is…anyone there?"

"Chloe. It's Matt. Matt Hanson."

Chloe's breath caught, her heart pounding beneath the form hugging cashmere sweater that so perfectly matched the pink tint of her glossed lips. Matt. As if she'd need his last name to know the voice that had haunted her dreams for the past five years. Her mind was already whirling, filling with questions – the main one being why her ex-husband's right hand man was calling her. The second centered around the butterflies taking flight in her belly at the sound of his voice.

There was something else… that undeniable sense of dread that accompanies an unexpected call.

"Matt. It's been a long time. Is… is everything okay?" That was Chloe, never one to beat around the bush. On most things, anyway. Her stomach tightened when Matt sighed and began to answer with halting words.

"I… I'm … Ah Chloe…" There was another moment of silence before he blurted out, "It's James…" Chloe noted the deep timbre of his voice held a definite mournful tone.

"What's happened, Matt? Where's James? Is he okay? Tell me he's okay!" Chloe's voice rose with the last sentence, tears filling her blue eyes. She may not be married to James anymore, but she still cared, loved him in fact. Just not the kind of love needed to make a marriage work. Not the way she loved… She shook her head, pushed a hand into her blond hair and leaned forward to where her elbows rested on the desk before her. She pressed the phone tighter against her ear. "Matt?"

"It's not good, Chloe. He rolled his truck down that hill by the curve about a mile from the house…"

She hadn't been there in years, yet Chloe knew the exact spot Matt was describing, knew it could be dangerous when the roads were bad if someone didn't know the road. But James knew that road, knew to be careful. What had happened? She thought of all the times he'd talked about having it reworked to lessen the danger. Obviously he never had.

Matt's words jarred her back to the unwanted news. "Doc Wilson… He said I'd better call you." He cleared his throat. Did that sniffling sound in the receiver mean Matt was crying?

"I'll let you know my flight information," she told him, tears beginning to roll down her cheeks.

"Chloe?"

"Yes?"

"Get here quickly."

The beeping in Chloe's ear let her know another call was coming in. She went straight from the devastating news about James to talking to her mom. Step mom, actually, though she was the only mother Chloe had ever known and she loved her as much as a true flesh and blood parent.

"Can you be at the airport in forty-five minutes, Chloe?" Claire hadn't even inquired as to how her daughter was or whether she wanted to make the trip. Chloe's get-to-the-point attitude was definitely *inherited*.

"I'm not sure. I… How did you know, Mom?" Her mind hadn't cleared from that initial moment when she first heard Matt's voice, mere thought and decisions becoming more difficult with the growing muddle.

"You're still listed as James' next of kin. Sheriff Dailey called to see if we would get hold of you and I figured when your line rang through to voicemail you were talking to Matt." The two women were both silent for a moment, each no doubt lost in her own thoughts. "I've already contacted Tom Miller. You remember Tom? He stayed here at The Meadows maybe six, seven years ago. His dream was to be a pilot even though his daddy wanted to steer him toward the helm of the company business. Investments brokerage, I think. Anyway, he flies private charters now and said he'd be waiting for you at the airport."

"But how'd you know I would agree to come?" Chloe choked out through her tears.

"I never doubted it for a second."

In her mind, Chloe could see an understanding smile turn Claire's lips upward. It was the same smile she used on the kids who spent time at O'Bryan Meadows – a place of exploration for privileged kids with dashed hopes of being able to live their own dreams instead of being molded into what their parents wanted for them. It was a place born out of Claire's life as a wealthy yet unhappy young woman, made to feel completely useless and unwanted by a father who couldn't see what a wonderful daughter he had because she didn't fit his ideal mold. Claire had almost taken her own life, just as Chloe's biological mother had. Only Elaine O'Bryan had succeeded. Chloe shivered. She longed to have Claire's gentle arms wrapped tightly around her just as they had been that night she explained why she had to leave James.

Chloe's dad, always analyzing/overly doting, met her at the top of the narrow steps as the door to the plane let down. He pulled her into a smothering hug before pushing her back so he could look at her.

"I'm all right, Daddy." Her red rimmed eyes and the tissue that had piled high during the hour and a half trip told a different story, but Garrett O'Bryan, gracious man that he was, chose to go along with Chloe's self-assessment.

"Let's get to the car so we can get you where you need to be. Claire managed to get clearance to bring it right up here. I don't know how she does it but I swear that woman can accomplish anything."

Chloe smiled at her dad's nervous prattle and obvious pride in his wife's capabilities. A stroke of pain sliced through her heart at the thought of her parents' love for one another. It was something she longed for and one of the main reasons she'd left James. She had hoped to move on and find what her parents shared.

Only what she'd wanted was back at James McCormick's Kentucky horse ranch.

With a great deal of effort, she pushed the thought away and followed Garrett down the plane's steps, glad her feet were back on solid ground. Flying had certainly never been a dream she'd harbored. Claire was waiting for her, standing beside the pilot, just a few steps away. Catching sight of her unleashed the flood of tears Chloe tried to hold back. Oh how they flowed, especially once she was in Claire's arms.

With a barely audible Thank You to Tom, Claire steered her to the waiting car and climbed into the back seat beside her. She pulled Chloe close, nestling the younger woman in her arms just as she'd done every time Chloe had ever needed her.

Chloe gasped causing Matt to turn toward the door. He'd been slumped forward in the chair beside James' bed, his head bent, hand wrapped around that of his friend. It was one of those moments that would be forever imprinted in her mind. She covered her mouth with her hand to smother a sob as he rose and started toward her. It wasn't until she was wrapped in his arms, pressed against him, that she let out a shaky breath.

Never had anything felt so wonderful and so awful at the same time as it did standing in James' hospital room in Matt's arms. The dull, gray-blue setting, meant to soothe, heightened her senses to the shadow of sickness and death, as did the sounds of the equipment monitoring James' vitals. Yet breathing in Matt's woodsy scent, melting into the security that came with having him hold her... Why did being near him always feel so right, even when she knew it was wrong?

"He's been asking for you." Matt loosened his hold – just enough for her to lean back so he could easily see her face. She saw the wariness in Matt's eyes at the hope within her own. "He fades in and out. Mostly he's out." He closed his eyes for a moment leaving Chloe to wonder what he was hiding. "They've got him so doped up … Doc called it 'keeping him comfortable.' Says that's all they can do."

Chloe shook her head, her eyes filling with tears.

"Shhh." A thumb dashed away the single drop that managed to escape to roll down her cheek. "We have to be strong – for James and for each other, okay?"

Chloe nodded, her lips quivering as she tried to smile.

"I'm glad you're here. James will be too," he whispered to her.

Unsure how to answer, she turned to a different line of conversation, though still on James. Otherwise she'd have to say she didn't want to be there, didn't want to face death or what she'd run away from almost five years ago. "I don't understand how this could have happened. He knew those roads, Matt. How could he have misjudged that turn?"

Matt turned his face away, gazing off at a vacant spot on the icy blue wall for so long Chloe was sure he wasn't going to answer, not that she'd really expected him to. Hows and Whys were never fully explained in life events.

He sighed loudly, tightened his hold, closing the distance between them. "Driving too fast. Distracted by..."

"By?" She didn't like the way he seemed to be dancing around without answering her.

He rolled his shoulders and his neck as if he was getting ready for a fight. "I suppose there's no reason to hide the truth from you now. But you need to remember something. You have to know that James loved you."

She nodded. She did know. That was why she'd left, left both men instead of coming between them and their thicker-than-blood friendship. She'd done that because she loved him.

"When we were in college there was this girl... Amy Cole." Chloe watched him travel back in time. "She ran with a pretty wild crowd, liked to party, and liked what she saw in the way of a future with James McCormick."

"What does this have to do wi..."

Matt placed a finger to her lips and continued. "When Amy turned up pregnant and swore the baby was his, James' parents stepped in and said no. You might remember Bart McCormick already had James' straight-backed, soft leather chair waiting in the office next to his."

She remembered James coming to O'Bryan Meadows. A young college sophomore, he was actually older than most of their guests, so after Claire met him she hired him as a summer employee. She'd then made sure part of his duties would have him sitting in on the sessions that would benefit him the most.

"Bart told James he'd work out an agreement to

help support the child if James would walk away. If not, he'd disown him and neither he nor the child would have anything."

"Was the baby his?" Chloe wasn't sure she wanted to know and yet had to.

"I honestly don't know. I'm sure it was possible." He looked almost apologetic. "We were young college boys, you know." Finger to forehead, he closed his eyes for a moment. "He looks an awful lot like James, Chloe."

Looks… He'd seen him? "You've seen him?"

"After James' dad died Amy called the ranch. Seems old Bart hadn't made provisions for after his death. I'm not sure I fully understand it, but James wanted to try to forge a relationship with the boy, a son who didn't even know or care that he existed until he convinced Amy to relocate to Clearview."

Chloe tried to process all she was hearing. The one thing she understood was why James had wanted to know his son. He'd wanted them to start a family right away. Chloe hadn't been ready, knew the marriage was a farce on her end. Now, guilt grabbed her. She'd denied him, even knowing the depth of his desire to be the father to his own child that his father never was to him. She tried to calculate the boy's age.

"He's fifteen," Matt answered as if he'd read her mind. "He has a lot of… issues." He ignored Chloe's raised eyebrows and continued. "I don't know what happened, Chloe, but James was on his way back from Clearview when he ran off the road. There's something else. Amy was with him. She died on impact."

"Where's their son?"

Matt was about to answer when her name floated to them, a raspy whisper from across the room.

Chloe and Matt both moved to the bedside. "I'm here, James." She spoke softly, leaning down so he could hear her, maybe feel her.

His eyes were muddy, lids heavy, though he managed to open them long enough to look at her. His bruised and cracked lips tried to form a smile.

"I'm a mess," he croaked.

"You always were, cowboy," she answered, squeezing his hand before slipping into the chair where Matt had sat.

"I'm glad you came." His words were broken, just like his body.

"You knew I would." A tear slid down her cheek.

He opened his eyes again, looking in Matt's direction before closing them again. "You told her about Robbie."

"Yeah," Matt answered.

"He's a good boy. Needs to know that." He squeezed Chloe's hand in a silent plea, his whole body tightening while he fought for shallow breaths of air. "So tired, Chloe."

"Just rest, James. Everything will be okay."

James nodded and turned his face away.

I know someday I will be thankful for this moment, she thought as she watched the shallowness of his breath increase until he took his last. Though for now she could feel only numbness seeping in. So many secrets. So many words left unsaid. Bending toward his hand within hers, she kissed the wedding ring he still wore and tasted the saltiness of her tears there. How would she ever get through this?

Matt's hand covered hers and James'. His arm around her shoulder, she leaned into him. Had it only been a few hours ago that she'd been dreaming of Paris?

Life would never be the same.

Talk With Me

"911. What seems to be the problem?"

What seemed to be the problem? Nothing really. Twenty-six year old Emma Westcott was on the *fast track* to an executive position. Even though it was in her father's company, she took pride in that she still had to earn every step to the next rung of the corporate ladder.

She was also on the cusp of marriage to the vice-president of that company; a man fifteen years her senior, he was touted as brilliant in business affairs and *the people* loved him. Her father continuously told her what a perfect husband his right hand man would make until she finally gave and began to date him. Now, her life planned, she floated along … absolutely miserable. Disappointment manifested itself as moisture pooled in the corners of Emma's eyes.

"You idiot. She's right there with the knife!. Watch out!" Guy yelled at the TV, involving himself in the police drama unfolding on the screen. "Can you believe that?" he asked Emma, his eyes never leaving the set, meaning he never saw her tears. Just another indication of his *great* people skills!

Emma nodded her head, though not in answer to his question. What she could not believe was that this was what she had to look forward to -- a lifetime of one mindless television show after another, him more caught up in their lives than in the flesh and blood woman by his side. She stood.

"You'll miss the ending." Again, his eyes did not leave the television.

"Can't wait. You'll have to tell me what happens." As if she cared. All she knew was she had to get out of there or there was going to be a real call to 911 and the problem was going to be that she'd murdered her fiancé!

Emma rushed to her room, grabbed her bag from the closet shelf and began to fish through it for a small piece of paper. Her organizational skills did not fail her and she had it in hand rather quickly. Clayton Reynolds, the torn sheet read, followed by a phone number.

"You need someone to talk with, Emm. Weddings are stressful but you're over the top. Come on. He's a great listener. I mean, it's not like you're cheating on Guy. Listening is what Clay does for a living." Emma replayed her best office mate's words in her head. She'd told her this man actually had several clients in the building -- women who merely needed a good listener. They'd go for a walk at lunch, or grab a bite to eat, maybe even meet for a coffee break or ice cream. They'd talk and he'd listen. It was that simple. Only Emma wasn't sure she could talk to a total strange, a man no less, about the issues in her life. He wasn't even a licensed therapist. What had Jen said? *Not therapy, just therapeutic. Get it off your chest.*

Emma had thought about that conversation every day for three weeks. Yet every time she'd picked up her phone to call, she'd chickened out. How could she talk to a strange man?!

Wasn't that what she really wanted? To talk with a *strange man*? Didn't she want to have a conversation with Guy? To have him notice her instead of the knife-wielding bimbo on the TV screen? Why couldn't he listen to her instead of a fictitious script?

Hands shaking, she dialed the number.

"Clayton Reynolds. Talk With Me!"

Emma was silent.

"Hello?"

Words refused Emma. No words meant no speaking.

"What seems to be the problem?"

Isn't that what the 911 dispatcher had asked on the show Guy was watching? The thought jarred Emma from her silence.

"I'm … sorry. I'm just a bit nervous."

"Happens all the time. What can I do for you?" His casual manner eased Emma's apprehensions a little. Not completely, but enough that she knew she really did want to set up an appointment to talk with him.

"Jen Wallace recommended that I call you…" her voice faltered slightly.

"Great! You interested in a walk and talk or you want to grab a bite? And when would be a good time for you?"

"How soon do you have an opening? For either?"

How much more desperate could she sound?

"I'm free this evening or …"

"This evening's perfect!" That's how much more. Emma groaned inwardly.

"How about dinner? Cost is $100 plus expenses. Does that work for you?"

"Yes. That works. Do you choose the place or do I?"

"Emm? Who are you talking with?" Guy peeked through the door. She hoped she didn't look as guilty as she felt.

"Hold please," she told the phone. "Business call." She smiled at Guy who merely nodded. "Your show get over?"

"Yes but they're running back to back episodes all evening long." He didn't wait for her response before returning to the TV.

Emma sighed.

"How about Maggie Jean's at 8:00?" the phone voice asked.

She glanced at the clock. Yes, 8:00 would do.

"I'm looking forward to meeting you."

Emma liked that. She was suddenly looking forward to the evening too. Now, how to deal with Guy? Her lips curled in an evil smile. Maybe she should put into action some of what she'd learned watching all crime shows. Get ready, she told herself.

"I'm going now," she told Guy when she returned to the living room.

"Emm? This is your house."

Emma's look mirrored the confusion on Guy's face. Maybe this wasn't the best idea. She'd just call and cancel...

"911. What seems to be the problem?" the TV blared. Guy's head swung back toward it.

"I have an appointment. You can let yourself out." And never come back, she wanted to add. Instead, she turned and walked out, his protests falling on ears deafened by his neglect. She would be ordering a lot of food knowing Mr. Reynolds' ears were all hers for however long it took them to eat their meal. She was starving for a different kind of fulfillment and she planned to get her money's worth. Every cent. No problem.

Secret Shame

I watched the boats drifting across the bay, jealous of their freedom, knowing it should have been mine as I began my senior year. They hoisted their sails to take advantage of the gentle breeze.

Advantage. That's what some would have said he'd taken of me. As for me, I wasn't sure. The guilt tried to squeeze in again. I chased it away. Was he to blame? Was I? I didn't know. Either way, I refused to feel shame. No. I hadn't known. Hadn't known anything other than the way he made me feel.

My flesh tingled with the memory of his touch. His trembling hands on my arms after he'd removed my wet shirt. The tickling sensations of his fingertips gliding up and across my back to move my hair away. The sweet softness of his lips against my neck, nibbling their way toward my ear where the sound of my name came to me on a breath, a whisper.

A gust of wind rushed around me, cooling skin that burned, yearned for him, even now when I knew it could never be.

He'd come to me one rainy night at the end of May. I'd just left the house of a new friend, foolishly walking home alone when the heavens opened up. From a cool evening sky filled with scattered clouds to a torrential downpour, it happened quickly, much like my life.

Much like the affair.

"Can I give you a ride?" he asked, rolling down the window just enough so that I could hear and see him. I hesitated, and he laughed. "I don't bite." He pushed open the passenger door, and I got in, still apprehensive but relieved to be out of the rain. My instincts told me I should not be there, yet something drew me. I was reminded of the moth and the flame.

It wasn't like he was a complete stranger. I'd met him at Allie's house. No, that wasn't true. I only saw him there. He hadn't stayed long. An older man, I assumed he had come to see Allie's father and left when he wasn't home.

I sighed, trying to push the angst away, and he smiled, just like he had at Allie. She'd seemed so at ease then, casually hugging him before she'd returned to my side, before we wandered off to meet and greet the others she'd invited to her end-of-school bash.

He asked my name and I told him, along with my address two blocks north, closer to the bay. We made small talk while he drove.

"Looks awfully dark," he said, pulling up in front of my parent's home.

"Yeah." My voice shook. I hated staying alone while my parents were away, which happened too often. I foolishly told him so and he offered to walk me in. I should have said no but agreed anyway, feeling more afraid of being alone than with him.

He helped me with the key and then the lights,

roaming around, closing the curtains I had forgotten to shut before I'd gone to Allie's.

"There." He smiled. "All better … except that you're shaking. You need to get out of those wet clothes."

The way he looked at me … I'd never felt desired, needed, never knew what it was to hurt with longing. How could I have known that one night would completely change my life? How could I have known that was how fate worked?

"I'm sorry," he said, though not until the morning light crept through the curtains. His words could not replace my innocence or squelch the loneliness I felt after he left my side. My feelings were unjust. Somewhere between that first kiss and our parting, I'd noticed his ring.

Weeks later, when I needed to talk to someone, I met his wife … and learned he had another child besides the one I held secret, growing inside of me. I'd gone back to Allie's house to tell her, feeling she was someone I could open up to. That's when she introduced me to her mom and dad. I knew then that I could never tell anyone about what had happened between me and the near-stranger that rainy night in May.

A sudden rain halted my retrospection. I turned to go back inside knowing the shelter of my home would not shield me from the drops that fell from my eyes.

What a cruel keeper fate was to have brought me heaven and hell all wrapped into one.

One more glance at the bay. The boats were lowering their sails, the unexpected rain cutting short their dreams of a perfect day.

What a shame.

Coasting Together

They'd ridden together so many times through the lush countryside of Terrington and the back roads of Cypress. Even the roads of Iowa which had great personal meaning to him. Yet, she'd never sat on the seat of a bicycle. She'd never experienced the exhilaration of the slow ride or contemplated the lives of those around as she coasted through cities, towns, and countryside at 15 mph. Things were so very different at this introspective pace. And they'd experienced the unfolding together.

How could that be? How could she have been there? Imagination, my friend. Daydreams. Fantasies. Desire, on both parts, born of needs unfulfilled in life. She was in his head and he was in hers. And together, they'd experienced all that this distracting illusion could offer. Together, they'd found peace in their ride through life, alone.

She was just 19 when the story began. He was 23. Both settling into lives resulting from having taken the wrong path somewhere along the way. Three more years and they'd meet for the first time and the vastness of their mistakes would begin to sink in. As their eyes met across the table where they'd been seated, both of them knew. The reality of diamond rings and wedding bands that had tied them to different people three years prior loomed between them even as their souls united in that stare.

She'd looked away. her heart beating so violently she was certain the two individuals sitting beside her could hear. He'd continued to look at her. His gaze appreciative, taking in every lovely detail, imprinting her forevermore into his mind.

At 22, Amanda Carlisle was indeed an exquisite creature to behold. Married to renowned playwright, Alexander Carlisle, she was a budding theater actress. Xander, as many called him, wanted to do a play about two men "finding themselves" as they rode across the country on bicycle, of all things.

Brian Matthews was an avid cyclist, as were the majority of the people in the room. Xander had assembled this conglomeration to "pick their brains" and to learn all he could about life on the seat of a bicycle. Amanda and two others had been assigned to talk with the six cyclists at table four. They were to learn all they could about the introspective parts of a slow cross country trek. Babs and Alan were both chatting with the cyclists. The pens that each held were practically flinging ink with the speed of their written words. Amanda's mind refused to form even one intelligent question. At last she turned back to see the man across the table smiling at her. With a jerky nod of his head he motioned for her to join him away from the others. Amanda politely excused herself to Babs and Alan's unchecked disdain.

She made her way to the little patio garden just beyond the west side French doors. Brian joined her seconds later. Little did she know she'd score big with Xander for the unexpected private meeting with the reining king of the cycling world. She did know, however, that the connection between them was undeniable. And, by the end of that day, the depth of that bizarre connection would come to light.

As Brian took a relaxing ride in the fading light of the evening sky he thought about the beautiful woman he'd met that afternoon. Across town in a moment of unexpected relaxed aloneness that very woman thought about the stunning cyclist. She closed her eyes and spoke his name.

"Brian," she whispered.

"Amanda?!" Her eyes snapped open as she was suddenly catapulted into his world, riding beside him through the streets of her city. They stared at one another in disbelief.

"Oh my! Wha what's go going on here?" she stammered.

Brian shook his head. He was as completely mystified as she was. They rode on in silence for some time. Shortly, they pulled to a stop next to a quiet stream.

"This is lovely!" she exclaimed as they removed their helmets and got off the bikes. "I've lived here all my life and never knew this place was here."

Brian nodded. "I've seen that happen time and again. You slow down and suddenly there's a whole new world before you." He smiled, enjoying himself as he watched her taking it all in. She began to walk closer to the water. She slipped on loose rocks and debris and he reached to steady her; but not before she knocked her knee on a large boulder on the bank.

"You okay?" He knelt beside her as she sank to the offending boulder to check the scrape.

"I'll live," she laughed. "Clumsy me. I could never have graced the stage as a ballerina." He smiled at her. They were eye level, eyes locked. His hand on her leg just below the wounded knee felt warm. His touch and his gaze combined made her breathing erratic. Instinctively, without thought, she leaned toward him, moistening her lips in anticipation.

"Mandy?" With a jerk she was sucked back into the sitting room chaise with Xander's voice calling to her. Confused and conflicted and just a little bit condemned she opened her eyes and looked about the dimly lit room. As Alexander entered Amanda twisted around so that her bared feet touched the plush Berman rug beneath the chaise.

"Ah! There you are darling." He was brimming with excitement as he knelt beside her much as Brian had done moments before. We've been working all evening compiling the information from the cyclists. You had quite an interview with that BMC guy. What a dream you are!" He leaned forward and kissed her cheek bumping her knee and she jumped. "Oh dear! Whatever have you done to yourself?" He asked, though his concern was apparently feigned, as he was already moving away without waiting for an answer. "Where's my Katie dear? I'm simply famished." Again he was speaking to her but not really. He was already moving out of the room looking for his "Katie dear", their housekeeper and cook all rolled up into one tight little middle-aged bundle Xander affectionately called his "other wife". Well, there were times when Amanda would gladly let her have him!

Amanda looked down. Her bruised knee proof positive the connection with Brian Matthews had not been a dream. "Oh Brian." She signed deeply. "I wish you were here."

"I am, Amanda!" the voice came clearly. Amanda looked around. She was quite alone.

"Where Brian?"

Brian's laughter filled her mind. "In your head apparently...and in mine."

"This is crazy. I don't understand." She was speaking to him but the words were all inside. They weren't audible to anyone but Brian; as were his words only to her.

"Amanda, don't be afraid." He could feel what she felt too. "It's a gift! We've been granted a strange and wonderful gift.

Amanda and Brian soon learned that it was during their quiet times that they were able to be together. During those times either could think of the other and mentally call. It was amazing how quickly they'd both set about simplifying their lives so that the quiet times were more easily found. That was much more difficult for Amanda. Brian was used to time away from it all as he trekked about on his cycle. But Amanda's life was riddled with activity. The theater, the parties, the endless stream of characters and unknown people traipsing in and out of the home she shared with Xander...and Katie. Two and a half years of mind training allowed them to easily connect now on a near daily basis for blissful rides through the country wherever Brian might be, or simple quiet togetherness. Sometimes they'd walk or even sit together on her private porch or in her salon. They'd talk about their lives and thoughts and concerns and dreams; always careful to avoid physical contact beyond simple hand holding.

But Xander's play, Coasting Together, had continued to gain increasing success, partly due to the little changes that Amanda suggested that kept it fresh. Xander had commented it was almost as if she truly knew what she was talking about from actual experience. Amanda would simply smile. In real life she'd never ridden a bicycle. Not even as a child!

As always happened, Amanda's life had become overly hectic once again with Xander's play, living his lifestyle, and the never ending acting classes he demanded she take for who knows what reason. One evening an amorous Xander had coaxed her into an early bedtime. It had been forever since he'd held her in his arms. She was optimistic.

"Xander," she began nervously though determined to push the issue. She was hopeful the fact that they'd just made love would have softened his demeanor enough that he would respond favorably. "When am I going to get to act in one of your plays?"

"Mandy, Mandy." He spoke in that theatrical tone she'd loved so much when they'd first met. Now she found it just shy of all out annoying and wished he'd save it for his followers and cronies. "These things take time. You know I want only the most perfect of roles for my best girl. It's here." He tapped his temple. "Formulating and taking shape. And speaking of shape..." His hands began to roam across her lovely figure and, without a definite answer, he'd made love to her again before drifting into his own world of contented sleep.

Amanda rolled away from him. Her heart breaking. She was far from contented, physically or otherwise. She wondered why she hadn't seen. Perhaps more so...what *had* she seen in Alexander Carlisle? As she lay there contemplating her life she heard him call to her.

"Brian?" Her mind confirmed that it was him. She smiled. Her eyes closed and she breathed steadily as she drifted impossibly across the barrier of reality to join him. "Kind of late for a ride isn't it?" she teased as they pedaled along the coastal highway together.

"Kind of early for bed," he poked back. She blushed which made him laugh. "You've been so busy lately I didn't know if you'd come." She nodded confirming that life had indeed been fast paced and hectic.

"Xander's cycling wonder is raving..." She tried to keep the bitterness from her voice.

"I see." He knew. They were in each others heads. There was no hiding.

She looked away so that he could not see the tears she blinked back. Again it was futile to hide. He could feel them. He knew her heart was breaking. That's why he'd called her.

Brian's life was so very different from hers. Amanda lived on the tails of Xander's dream kite; the one he'd promised she'd fly on at his side. Brian made his own way. The owner of his own line of cycling gear, he now traveled the country promoting his own products. And quite successfully too. His helmets and other safety products were top of the line and in high demand. Especially after he won one endurance challenge after another using, you got it, BMC Gear.

By all accounts, Brian Matthews was a success. Only problem, his personal life fit his initials. B.M.....a pile of crap. He'd married at 23. Sandra Kingsley, a fellow cyclist. Pretty girl. Self assured with a smile that could melt any man's heart. It had certainly turned his to molten mush. The problem was, the gold band he'd given her hadn't stopped her from turning that smile on others. He knew that every time he left on one of his promo tour another local would be consumed in the lake of her seemingly insatiable passionate fire.

Brian had tortured himself with it at first, even

threatening to leave her. She'd reminded him of how BMC was part hers and, at the time, the dream could not have withstood the split or the bad press. He'd retreated to his one true love, his bicycle. Then he'd met Amanda and their extraordinary ability to meet and connect mentally presented itself. And life took on a macabre illusional reality made tolerable by those meetings. Each of the two participants lived for those moments when life allowed them the gift to find one another.

"You okay?" Brian asked as Amanda tensed up unexpectedly.

"Shh," she said laying a finger against her lips. They stared at one another. Their breaths steady, they rode in unison. Slowly she began to relax. He could see the tension leaving her body, feel it. He returned the smile she offered to him though no explanation was given....or needed. Xander had rolled over, bumping into her, threatening to dissolve the ride. It had happened before, especially in the beginning. But the years had taught them and she'd learned ever so well how to control the strange force that brought them together.

Contentedly they rode; talking, laughing, sharing. Their time together was an insane escape that kept them both sane. They both wanted it. Both needed it.

Twelve years Amanda had waited for her part in one of the critically acclaimed Alexander Carlisle plays. Twelve years! Not one little part. And he'd refused to allow her to take parts from others, although they were frequently offered. Instead of helping her to fulfill her dreams as he'd promised, he had, in effect, killed them. At 31 she felt washed up professionally.

And now, Xander had informed her he was leaving her. Amanda was in shock, not because she wanted him to stay necessarily, but because she'd been blindsided. Their lives had grown so completely far apart that she hadn't even noticed all the time and attention he had begun to lavish on and receive from one Victoria Billingsly. Victoria, it seemed had been offered a part in Xander's latest masterpiece. Apparently she'd played the part marvelously as well as playing herself right into his bed. She was expecting his child; something Amanda had always believed unimportant to him.

Amanda's chest began to heave as she fought back the emotional barrage that threatened to engulf her.

"Mandy, Mandy," Alexander began. "It's all so right. You'll see. You'll come to understand..." He tried to take her in his arms.

Eyes wide with disgust and confusion she pushed against him and wheeled away. "Get out!" she screamed.

"Now Mandy, darling. Don't worry. Xander will take care of you always. Always my darling." Again he moved toward her.

"Don't you touch me." She picked up a vase and hurled it at him, barely missing his pretty inflated head. "Go!" she growled.

"I understand, darling. You need some time." And with that he slipped from the room and, pretty much, from her life.

"Amanda? Amanda come to me." She heard Brian's voice through the mist.

"Brian!" Yes, she needed Brian and he knew. "Oh, Brian..." Suddenly she was before him, her mind still filled with a thick fog. As she stared at him tears began to trickle down her cheeks. Slowly she shook her head, turning it back and forth.

Brian reached for her hand and pulled her to him, enfolding her in the comfort of his arms as she buried her face in his chest and sobbed. He held her, quietly stroking her back and hair, waiting.

As control returned she turned her face up to him and smiled weakly. "It still hurts and I don't know why. I should be happy to be free..." her voice broke. Brian nodded, unshed tears forming in his own eyes. Failure was failure even if it opened doors for better things to come. He also understood what it was like to be usurped by another. Or, as was the case with his wife, another and another and another. As he stared down into the tear-streaked face of the only woman he'd ever truly loved and been loved by, a smile began to form inside and out.

She looked at him in wonderment unable to read his feelings. He placed the palm of his hand on her cheek and wiped the tears away with his thumb. Lowering his hand his fingers brushed across her beautiful lips.

"Yes," she whispered and he lowered his face to

where their lips were centimeters apart.

"I love you, Amanda," he whispered as he kissed her softly. "I always have."

"I know," she answered in her mind.

Laughing he attempted to pull away but she refused to let him go. The kiss deepened and she pressed against him, her mind and her body reeling with raptured togetherness like nothing she had ever felt before.

"Amanda! If we don't stop soon I won't be able to," he said pulling away at last. Breathless, they stared at each other. "I want us to wait....until we're married."

Amanda was sure her heart would burst with the joy that consumed her. "Oh Brian! We'll be together...for real. Us." As Amanda reached up to kiss him the illusion dissolved.

"Brian?" she called then called again and waited. "Brian?" she called louder and then more frantic followed by a confused whisper.

Amanda sat down on the chaise. "Oh Brian." She'd never felt as completely alone as she did at that moment. Brian was gone from inside her and she had no idea where to find him in the real world. She didn't even know where he lived. She'd never needed to.

Amanda fixed herself a drink and went out to sit on the porch of her little rented cottage. She'd received word. Her divorce was final. She felt happy enough considering she was alone. Completely alone.

"Oh Brian," she whispered into the fading light of the evening sky. "If only you were here with me..."

"I am here, Amanda." She sat up straight as Brian's voice came to her. She placed her hand on her chest but could feel nothing. Disappointed she sat back against the bench realizing she'd wanted it so badly she'd imagined it. She closed her eyes.

"Amanda," he called to her, his voice a soft whisper. Her eyes snapped open. Brian stood before her in full cyclist gear. He smiled at her and held out his hand. Uncertain, she reached out and was met with a flesh and blood hand that pulled her to him.

"How Brian?" He tapped his temple then his heart.

"The day my divorce became final I set out to find you. My heart brought me here." He smiled and pointed to her heart.

She wanted to tell him his story was impossible and there was no way she'd believe it. But considering their life together so far, she knew anything was possible as long as you're willing to believe. Even the impossibility of their love bringing him to her.

The Key to Happiness

That did it! They'd done it again with their laughter and hugs. It had zipped the spring right out of my step ... again. I was sick of it!

He smiled at me and looked away as I walked by. She said hi, her eyes filled with playfulness. She'd been teasing him about something. I nodded, thinking I'd be all happy camperfied too if I had a guy like that. I sighed and turned up the walkway to my place. I was glad our units weren't side-by-side so I didn't have to share a stoop with them or listen to their happiness through the walls.

Huh. I hadn't noticed the railing was loose. I'd have to report that to the landlord ... which meant a call to my dad. He owned the building. He'd lived there years before while attending the university just down the street. He'd worked his way through school selling bits and pieces of his artwork and playing curator at the Campus Gallery – where I now worked.

Dad had painted and given art lessons in the very unit that I now called mine. And, when opportunity had knocked, long after he'd gotten his big break, he'd bought the building ... and the Gallery. He'd said it was nostalgia. More likely he knew they were great investments and my future.

Hearing them talking by the curb as I tried to get my key to fit brought me back. His laughter floated around me not unlike the leaves that glided down from the changing trees. I felt the goose bumps prickling my skin like they did every time I heard him. I wanted to turn around and take a peek, but I didn't because I knew what I would see. Him. Her. Together. I wondered if there would ever be anyone like him for me.

I tried to blow my bangs out of my eyes so I could see what I was doing. Darn that key! I fumbled with the bag of groceries, overfilled of course. I couldn't blame the store. One bag, I'd said, thinking it would be easier. Wrong! The thing was top-heavy and kept trying to topple no matter how I balanced it. Yep. There went my apples. I let out a disgusted groan as my forehead smacked against the door jam.

"Can I help?"

I couldn't move. It was him. Talking to me! I could see him out of the corner of my eye, standing there, his beautiful face poking out from the neck of his fisherman's sweater – right where it should be. He was holding my apples.

I should move. I should say something. Oh God! Help me! I could feel the nervous twitch in my stomach. Please don't let me puke on his shoes!

"Thanks," I heard myself say instead as I somehow managed to push myself off my front door. "I can't seem to get my key to work." I bit my lower lip then tried to twist my mouth into something that resembled a smile. I was either successful or looked ridiculous because he laughed.

"Your name's Paige, right?" He traded me an apple for my key.

I nodded, overwhelmed by the fact that he knew my name.

"I'm Michael." He smiled again, the dimples in his cheeks constricting my lungs until I wasn't sure but I think they forgot how to breathe. He held up my key. "I think your key might fit better in your door than it does mine." He laughed at my horror as I stepped back to confirm what he'd said.

I groaned, though I was thinking how much I liked his laugh. It was a hearty sound that made me laugh too.

"You have a great smile. You don't use it nearly enough."

I blushed. My cheeks turning as red as the apples he returned to my bag right before his fingers rakes across my forehead, pushing back the crop of bangs that still hung in my eyes.

"That's better. I wasn't sure if they were green or blue. It's hard to tell from a distance."

My face was locked in a perpetual smile. "They're blue," I said, "with a hint of green." It hit me. He'd obviously taken note of my appearance some time before.

He traded the key for my top-heavy bag of groceries and followed me to my door – the right door. Without reserve or an invitation, he slipped inside. He knew exactly where he was going. The layout of every unit was the same.

"Wow!" He'd taken it upon himself to start unloading the bag. "Planning a feast?"

I laughed. I liked to cook and I told him so. I could see the longing in his eyes.

"You should invite a starving artist to dinner sometime." He was fishing.

"You know one?" I already knew the answer. I'd seen him sitting outside his place with his art supplies every Saturday at noon for the past three months. He laughed. So did I. And then I sobered. "Don't you think your girlfriend might mind?" My stomach knotted. Hadn't they been hugging at the curb as I'd walked by?

His laughter filled my kitchen. "Are you talking about Carrie?" he asked through mirth that filled his eyes with tears.

I shrugged and handed him a tissue. I didn't understand his laughter and I certainly didn't know her name.

"Carrie's my sister. We're rooming together to save money. Her husband's playing at minor league ball while we both take classes at the university. With his pay, her part-time job, and my art scholarships, we manage the two bedroom pretty well. Can't beat the location."

I wanted to agree but my voice had left me. My head refused to move. This was too good to be true. My mistake seemed to be the key to happiness and it felt even better than the noonday sun shinning down as I'd walked along longing, listening to the crackle of fallen leaves beneath my feet on a near-empty sidewalk.

Healing Words

Sam released the handle of the hospital room door, his fingertips slipping from the cold metal with the realization he had no business being there. Sure, he was a doctor. Yes, he'd performed the medical procedures in the operating room that had most likely saved the life of the patient inside.

And changed it dramatically.

His heart hurt knowing hers would when she finally awakened to find the tiny life inside her gone. Damn, he'd hated to do that, but the bleeding... Car wreck victims were never easy to treat, though he'd bet a week of his physicians' salary that part of this young woman's trauma was suffered well before she'd wrapped her little car around a tree three days prior.

Sam had visited her room every day since, hoping for news she'd awakened, knowing there was no medical reason she had not.

Except a reason to want to.

That thought made him wonder if somehow she already knew about the baby, about the fact that she'd never have the chance to carry another one. Day and night since he'd treated her in the ER thoughts about her had plagued him. What was her story? What had she been through? And the worst: had her wreck been an accident?

No. He refused to believe she'd intentionally ran off the road into the shallow ravine, her car rolling twice before bending in half when it was stopped by the thick trunk of a tall tree. But if she'd been speeding, her tears mixed with the rain … visibility would have been limited, control lessened. What was her story?

Sam shook his head. He shouldn't care. Being impassionate, impersonal was Med 101. Getting involved in a patient's life was simply not allowed.

"Everything okay, Doc?"

Sam turned toward the gently inquiring voice, returned the smile she offered him, knowing her age-wisened eyes missed nothing. She didn't ask why he was there. Perhaps she knew the reason even better than he did.

He nodded and ran a hand through the dark hair cropped short on his head before sucking in a deep breath to answer.

"You haven't been in yet, then." Wanda Velory, the head nurse of Dana Covey Women's Hospital spoke before he did. "No change, though she's doing just fine thanks to your handiwork." She paused then shook her head. "Still no visitors. Pretty, young thing like her, you'd think her room would be full. At least she will be once the scrapes and bruises heal." She looked off into the distance before continuing, "Makes no sense, really."

She'd voiced his thoughts. "What about her parents? Or…the baby's father?"

Wanda shook her graying head. "Not a word. Haven't even inquired about how she's doing. None of them. Parents were notified. Boyfriend, it seems, is nowhere to be found." She was watching him again, imploring him with those gray-blue eyes. "Not very often that I recommend getting involved, Sam. I know it goes against all our medical training, but I have a feeling she could sure use a friend and I'm guessing you could too. You've done nothing but work since Laura left…"

"That's not true!" he interrupted, his lips thinning into a tight line. "What about my girls?"

Wanda chuckled and shook her head again. "Don't take offense, Hon. But they're six and four. Dinner dates at McDonalds with your daughters a couple of nights a week isn't exactly what I meant. That kind of interaction and socializing isn't the only thing you need and we both know it. You're looking for something, Sam. Even if you don't want to fess up to it." She smiled, not the smile of one who has caught someone else with his hand in the candy jar, but a compassionate, understanding upturning of the lips. "What do you think keeps drawing you back here?" She patted the firmness of his upper bicep, covered by the starched white dress shirt usually hidden beneath a knee length doctor's coat. "Perhaps the attention of a new friend would help Emma wake up."

Emma. Not just a patient lying still in a sterile bed beyond the wooden door, but a person with a name and a life she needed to live. If nothing else, perhaps he could offer her a sense that someone cared. He was a healer, and if that's what it took…

Sam knew it was an excuse to make himself feel better about wanting to be there. He didn't understand it but he felt some kind of bond with this young patient; no doubt one-sided since she'd been unconscious since shortly after the paramedics had brought her in. But perhaps in helping her, somehow he'd begin to heal. Heaven knew he needed it.

Laura's sudden proclamation she no longer loved him, that she was leaving and taking his girls had torn him apart. At 36, Sam was sure his life was over. And it was, in a sense. At least the life he'd known, expected to always be there. He'd thrown himself into his work and making the most of the two times a week he had to spend with his daughters, when work didn't detain him. He'd shut down to keep his heart from hurting and had done a pretty good job of not feeling until Emma Sanders had rolled into the ER on one of his rotation nights. 23 years old, a car wreck victim who looked more like she'd had the crap beaten out of her than she did someone who had tangled with metal and wood. And now she refused to wake up. There was something going on with her beyond whatever it was that had thoughts of her tugging at his heart and taking over his mind. She needed a reason to go on every bit as much as he did.

"Thanks, Wanda." Without waiting for a response from the older nurse, Sam pushed through the door to Emma's room. He froze as he stepped inside, his heart hammering while that little voice told him it was crazy to get involved in a stranger's life. Especially an unconscious stranger who had been his patient. He knew he should leave, even went so far as to reach for the door handle again. But he couldn't. She looked so … alone laying there, the bleeping of the monitors the only thing breaking the silence. Tomorrow, he would bring flowers and maybe balloons to liven up the room. Yes, that's what he'd do, he thought, nodding his head as he moved closer to her.

"Emma." It seemed peculiar to be calling her by her name. "I'm Dr. Walsh. Sam Walsh." He lowered his tall frame into the seat beside her bed and reached for her hand. "A colleague recommended a little game, a word game. I thought we'd give it a try," he fumbled, feeling funny. He decided not to mention the game was to help work the brain, get it firing, and hopefully help her wake up. Instead, he pulled out his phone, pulled up the words and began to read them and their definitions until he was too tired to go on.

Each afternoon Sam returned to Emma's room to play the word game, talk to her, and even read to her from a paperback they'd found among her belongings at the wreck site. It was the 6th day. No signs of waking. Sam was beginning to feel the strains of discouragement. He plopped down beside her bed. He was tired. Laura had been irritable when he called to check on the girls and make sure she remembered he was picking them up that evening for an overnight stay. It meant cutting his visit with Emma short, though he doubted she'd miss him much.

The thought made him chuckle, a low sound that rumbled through his chest and ended with a groan. He leaned forward, his head drooping, fingers pushing through his thick hair.

"Emma, Emma, Emma..." Sometimes he wished he could just go to sleep and block out the world for a while.

But he couldn't. He let out a long, loud exhale and pulled out his iPhone, pressing the buttons to get to the list of words. F-words. For some reason that made him laugh again. He was glad he had the next day off since it was pretty obvious he needed the break.

May as well get started, he thought. "Facile: Appearing neat and comprehensive by ignoring the complexities of an issue; superficial. Frenetic: Fast and energetic in a rather wild and uncontrolled way. Fastidious: Very attentive and concerned about accuracy and detail..." He sighed again. This wasn't working, at least for him.

Sam leaned over and grabbed Emma's book that remained exactly where he'd left it the day before. "Claire sat down on the edge of her bed to remove her shoes. She laid her phone on the nightstand next to the two waiting pill bottles then pulled off her earrings which she placed next to the phone. Putting a hand over her heart, she reached for the bottles with her empty hand and realized for the first time in a very long time she hadn't thought about the hurt inside for many hours. Maybe Garrett really was an angel. She considered the idea. Either way he'd altered the course of her life. She opened the nightstand drawer and dropped the bottles inside. A sudden wave of exhaustion engulfed her. Garrett was right. It was late. Claire looked at her phone and shook her head as she realized she hadn't gotten his number. Now the true question… was *he* a man of *his* word? Would he show on Sunday morning?"

Interesting how crossing paths with another can alter ones life. Sam put down the book, reached for Emma's hand and squeezed. "I don't know if I'll be here for the next couple of days, Emma. I have my rotation in the ER coming up and tomorrow I'll have my girls until late afternoon…"

Sam jumped, his eyes jerking down to look at their hands. She'd squeezed his hand. She had, hadn't she? His mind raced. What had he said? He wouldn't be there … ER rotation … day off … No! His girls.

"My… my girls are four and six." He laughed softly. "They're a handful…" There it was again. Yes! "Kimberly, Kimi, is the oldest. Has dark hair, full like mine only long and wavy. Sara looks more like her mom…"

Emma groaned a little. He felt more than saw her twisting beneath the sheets.

"I… I only get to see them a couple of times a week now…"

Her eyes fluttered several times then opened. He could tell she was unable to focus on him but he stood, smiling down at her just the same.

"Welcome back," he whispered, his free hand stroking the sandy tangles away from her face. She tried to return his smile though frowned instead before attempting to reach for the tube between her still-swollen lips. The loosely tied restraints, there for that very reason, checked her motion. Light blue eyes implored him to help her, just as they had right before she'd been taken into the operating room that night in the ER.

"It's okay. I'll get the nurse to see about getting that out." Without releasing her hand he pressed the button that would summons a nurse. He hoped it would be Wanda.

Sam had planned to leave after letting Emma know he'd be AWOL for a few days, even though he still had an hour and a half before time to pick up his girls. But her sudden awakening had been met with a flourish of activity and excitement. Sam knew he'd be even more exhausted when the adrenaline rush whooshed from his body. Hopefully he'd be home with the girls playing with some of their favorite toys in front of the fireplace. He smiled. Children were so resilient. They seemed to be adjusting better than the adults. His chest swelled knowing talk of his girls had been the catalyst to bring Emma back. She'd have to meet them…

"My baby?"

Her words cut through his thoughts like a dull sword. No one answered her, including him, even though he felt her eyes on him. His face contorted and he shook his head no after she mouthed *please*. She turned back to stare at the ceiling, a single tear welling in the corner of her eye, releasing to roll down the side of her face. That single tear broke his heart.

Emma didn't want to talk about why her parents never came to see her, refused to speak about the baby's father, or whether there had been any foul play prior to the accident. All of that leading Sam to believe more than ever there was something going on and that she needed someone by her side. That, and the fact that he'd become quite attached to her during her hospital stay, brought about an offer that surprised them both. He didn't know where their relationship was headed, but he did have a spare bedroom in a big, lonely house where she was welcome to stay for as long as she needed. To his relief, Emma accepted the offer, though he realized on her part it may have been more out of having no place else to go. It didn't matter. He'd have her close by and that seemed to provide a healing they both needed and perhaps in time he'd have the opportunity to share with her the words that had begun to form in his heart; words that let him know the wounds inflicted by his own life were healing. Just like the woman in Emma's book, happenstance had changed his life. Opportunity knocked and he had, gratefully, opened the door to let her come inside.

So Right

They were always together. Casey, Michael, and Steven. The three amigos. For as long as anyone could remember it had been the three of them. Born weeks apart, living streets apart, they'd learned to walk together, started school together, driven their first cars together, even went on their first dates together. They'd been there for one another when teams were not made, relationships dissolved, for every disappointment life threw at them. One could definitely say they were comfortable with one another and they were as comfortable together with all three or just two of them. No matter what, they always felt so right.

So when it happened, it really wasn't surprising and it definitely didn't feel wrong. Casey and Michael were spending a lazy afternoon together at his house. Steven was working. He was due to join them in an hour.

When their fingers touched, and even entwined, it seemed okay. They'd held hands before. Even when he leaned against her and playfully sniffed her, she felt no concern. He was met with a hard shrug of her shoulder as she pushed into him and he grabbed the sleeve of her shirt in his mouth.

"What do you think you're doing?" She narrowed her eyes at him, twisting to try to release herself. "You know you can't win. I've always been able to take you then send you home cryin' ta mama. How embarrassing," she taunted, "Mikey Pooh....beaten by a girl!"

"You're a girl?" His face registered feigned shock. "I never noticed. "The game proceeded as usual. Casey knew exactly where this was headed. How many times in the past had they wrestled? How many times had it been all out war, especially when the three of them were involved?

As he advanced upon her, his eyes filled with mischief, he added, "Uh, Case…in case you hadn't noticed…we're at my house and Mama ain't home. Nowhere to run to and no one to save you Princess Not!"

Casey screamed and dissolved into delighted childish laughter as he captured her and she began to fight back with all her might. She even managed to get away and ran to the back of the couch. He jumped over causing her to scream again and make a run, but she was caught. In the middle of the living room floor they collapsed, laughter and fun permeated the room. He sat astride her, had her hands pinned above her head.

"Give!" he commanded as she writhed beneath him attempting to free herself. She shook her head no. The blond hair splayed about behind her on the floor shimmered. Her blue eyes sparkled. She moistened her lips and Michael was suddenly engulfed with a desire for her. Without warning he leaned down and kissed her.

From inches above her face, he stared at her. Casey. His Casey. *Their* Casey was stunningly beautiful and he'd never noticed. She'd always been just one of them.

She looked back at him. Silently her eyes darted about his face. Confusion reigned. He could feel her heart beating rapidly against his chest.

"Case, I'm sorr…"

Then she surprised them both by jerking her hands free and pulling his head back to meet hers.

"Oh, Casey," he whispered as he kissed her mouth, her neck, his hands beginning to roam over her. She said nothing, simply led him, allowed him. It felt so right.

Steven's shift ended early. The day had been challenging. Not only was it busy but his boss, Harold Snider, had called him in to offer him a full-time position. A job doing what he loved, working with planes, all the time…forever. Of course graduation would have to come first. And what of Casey and Michael? They'd all made plans to go to college together. What would his amigos think if he backed out and broke up the team? Yet here was the offer of a lifetime. Harold had even said they'd foot part of the bill for him to attend the local college. Granted it wasn't as prestigious as a University. But he'd have help with the cost, doing what he loved….and he'd be around to help his mom. Since his dad had died things had been rough. There never seemed to be enough to make ends meet.

Steven smiled as he thought of how his two closest friends had been right there beside him. He didn't want to let them down. He needed to think. Harold told him to take his time, go on home, and let it sink in. He'd ran a hand through sandy brownish/blond hair, winked a blue eye in thanks and ended his shift early. It was a quiet, pensive drive across town to meet his friends.

He pulled into Michael's drive. Casey's car wasn't there but he knew she was. He could feel her. She must have walked over. He smiled as he thought of that third amigo. Little Casey Remington. She'd turned into quite a lovely young lady and, as of late, he'd begun to have some different feelings for her. He was having to work awfully hard to put them down. He thought of the day and shook his head. Why did there always have to be such jagged edged forks in the road of life? And not one with just two tines of decisions but 3 or 4 and none of them clean cut and dried. He wanted it to all be clear.

Stepping from the car, he headed for the side gate as usual. He'd let himself in through the back slider for as long as he could remember; always been welcomed in Michael's home. But the site that met him that day seared itself into his mind and across his heart. As he slid open the door and stepped inside, his adjusting eyes took in Casey and Michael scurrying in their attempts to right wronged garments. Casey's blue eyes met his then looked away, her head hung in shame. Tears of regret and confusion dropped one by one onto the floor beneath. Oh what sheer betrayal! She'd cheated on her best friend with her best friend. She felt awful. How had she let this happen?

Without a word, Steven turned to go. Michael was on his feet instantly, nearly toppling Casey as he went after the third amigo. He caught him as he rounded the corner of the house.

"Steve, I…"

"What?!" Steven turned on him. "You want me to stand here while you say sorry? Didn't mean it? Not sure what happened? You think any of that matters?"

Michael shook his head. Nothing he could say or do could change what had happened. He stepped back and watched his lifelong friend go.

Back inside, a fully dressed Casey sat on the sofa, waiting. Her hopeful eyes watched Michael's return. He shook his head and dropped to the couch beside her.

"What are we going to do Michael?" she asked as she leaned against him in an attempt to find comfort in the one way they always had…each other. Michael put his arms around her, holding her tightly; he shook his head yet again. Lightly he kissed the top of her head fleetingly thinking to himself that she smelled really good. Their little princess.

He attempted a joke. "Guess you really are a girl after all."

She responded with a quiet little laugh. "Guess I was. Now I'm a woman…without a friend."

Two weeks later the three amigos graduated. They put on a plausible show for their parents who had begun to wonder why the trio had been together so little the final half month of their high school lives. Casey felt hot tears stinging her eyes as she sat between the two men that meant the most to her; especially when each of them reached over and took a hand. Steven brought her hand to his lips and kissed her knuckles. Casey was surprised.

"I've missed you," he whispered, leaning toward her. She smiled and squeezed his hand tightly before glancing at Michael who was staring straight ahead. He'd seen though. He knew Steven loved her every bit as much as he did.

Michael burst into Casey's frilly purple princess bedroom. "I hear you're sick. You never get sick. You okay?" He plopped down on the bed, the motion causing Casey to grab her lurching stomach.

"Ugh!" She rolled her eyes. "If I throw up one more time...I can't seem to shake this stomach bug."

"Been to the doctor?" he asked patting her peaked cheek. "Poor baby."

"Don't baby me, Michael. I'm older than you!" she teased through yet another bout of nausea. "I go tomorrow. Didn't want to but..."

"By a week only you're older! Case, you don't think..." The words hung between them with no others spoken. She looked away. It was a thought she'd been battling to suppress. After a moment she started to answer but was interrupted by Steven's grand entrance.

"Hey Princess Not. Heard you'd been driving the porcelain bus for more than a few days now." He playfully pushed Michael and dropped a small brown sack on the bed beside Casey. Her breath caught when she looked inside. "Cover your ears Mikey. Casey's gotta go potty and she doesn't want anyone to hear."

Sticking her tongue out at both of her best friends she climbed from beneath the purple sea and took the brown sack to her private bathroom.

"Dead or alive?" Steven called through the closed door when she hadn't returned after plenty of time.

"Now what do you think?!" she called back. They all knew the answer already. The two boys also knew Casey was crying. They looked at each other. Michael shrugged.

Steven called again, "Come out Princess. We'll figure it out. We're the three amigos." The door slowly opened. Casey collapsed in Steven's arms, sobbing. Michael joined them and the three best friends held each other and cried together.

Casey made the most beautiful bride. Michael's heart pounded as he watched her father walk her down the aisle and place her hand in his. With a deep breath he kissed her cheek.

"I love you, Casey," he whispered as he turned and walked her the last couple of steps to a waiting

Steven. The three embraced before Michael stepped to the side. It just seemed so right.

That night as they lay together for the first time, Steven kissed Casey's belly. No one knew but the three of them. "I hope she looks just like her beautiful mother," he said. Casey smiled.

The baby did not look like her mother. Jacob Michael Dorsey looked exactly like his father, especially as he grew. Even Michael's wife, Cindy, would joke that Jacob looked more like their Jesse than he did his own sister.

"Where'd those dark eyes and hair come from?" People would tease, innocently citing the affection the three amigos had for each other as having jumped barriers. Arm in arm in arm the three friends, now partners in the business world as well, would smile. They were satisfied and happy. Each knew they'd done the right thing because life felt so right.

Dance With the Enemy
~ The Chase

Her chest heaved with every breath, straining against the bodice of the silk gown. Silk - supposedly spun by the gods, meant to entice as it fell in revealing layers over the satiny skin of young ladies waiting for the men for whom they were chosen. To Elenya it only impeded her escape through the thick brush. She pushed the hood of the cloak-like dress from her head, releasing a magnificent mass of red tresses that matted against the trickle of sweat running down her back, now bare from the unusual cut of the dress.

What a waste. She thought of her trip to the courts as well as the expensive fabric and the excitement that had surrounded picking it out, fashioning it into a body-covering masterpiece that represented her future, her dreams. Her family should have saved their reserves, her destiny decided many years ago by higher authorities anyway. The only thing she'd needed to entice her warrior was her scent. Or was it his scent? She wasn't sure, knowing only that she'd been marked, ceremonially injected with his blood as a child to belong to him when her *season* came – though neither of them would know the other until the appointed time.

Even aware that she'd been marked and her future assured, Elenya was no different from the other girls who dreamed of a lifetime dance with one of the elite warriors of the court. It meant she and her family would return to the luxury of the circle of the chosen once she came of age.

Only the moment Elenya realized the Masters had matched her with Tahruk, she knew that would not be the case. Tahruk! Why? Their families had been enemies for generations. There had to be some mistake. She knew she had to find a way, to find someone who could make it right. Her only chance was to get to the house of the Masters.

Ignoring the aching in her legs and lungs, she refused to pay heed to the burning of the cuts and scratches inflicted on her limbs by the cruel sticks and whipping grasses. She would not cry over the sounds of her beautiful black dress ripping as she ran. She glanced down at what now looked like shredded rags. Careful! Taking her eyes off the terrain could have made her lose her footing and then it would all be over. She could hear him not far behind. Only her slight size lent itself to her ability to outmaneuver him through the dense brush.

Elenya longed for the smooth desert sands of home. Life had seemed so promising then as she'd played and worked beside her sisters, making sure they stayed within earshot of the voices of the elders whose sole purpose was to protect the future of their people: her.

There it was! She could see the house of the Masters. Elated that her uncanny sense of direction had led her right to it after seeing it only once, she was concerned about the clearing that lay before her. Her pursuer would be unhindered.

A man opened the house door causing hope to surge, hurling Elenya forward. He had to be one of the Masters.

"My Lord! My Lord!" she screamed, garnering the attention of men she hadn't realized were there. Panic rose as they converged on her, though she dodged them, stopping only when she had thrown herself at the feet of Dahru, the head Master. Only when her arms wrapped around his legs did she dare glance back at the warrior who crossed the clearing at a more casual pace. Anger burned behind his eyes, their dark depths glowing within his sun-bronzed face. Even as she shivered, she was unable to break away from his gaze. She felt the pull of the marking as she watched him run a hand through his night-black hair. She fought against it.

"Tahruk? What is the meaning of this?" asked the voice above Elenya's head.

"I wish to know that as well, Lord Dahru." As the warrior spoke, his chin tilted upward and he sniffed the air.

Dahru looked at his brethren before addressing the other man. "She ... the woman is yours then?"

Tahruk nodded. He glared down at the beauty who attempted to scoot around the strong legs of her refuge, seeing her clearly for the first time. His anger spiked as he took in the honeyed cinnamon hair, sun-kissed ivory skin, and soft pink lips, full and enticing. He watched as Dahru's hands locked on her arms and lifted her to stand before him instead. She tried to look over her shoulder. Again, the unmistakable pull warred against her fear.

"Look at me." The firm voice denoted care. He smiled as he wiped some of the grime from her face. "Why would you do this?" When she didn't answer, he added, "What is your name, maiden?"

Her voice trembled as did her body. Gone was the brave woman who had fled her warrior. "I am Elenya Avenille of the Aleone Drille," she answered quietly, listening for certain response from behind.

Having recognized her by her appearance as the Aleone woman, hearing her speak it pushed the warrior beyond reason. "Aleone!" he roared. Elenya pressed herself against Dahru. His strong arms encircled her small frame.

Dahru silenced the younger man with a raised hand, though the outburst was understandable. The disdain felt by the two Drilles, one for the other, had been passed down from generation to generation.

"There must be a mistake…"

"No." Dahru stopped Elenya's verbalization of the thought that echoed through many heads. "The Masters do not make mistakes. You must go with this man and fulfill the obligations imposed by the marking."

"I… I am afraid…" Elenya whispered before looking over her shoulder at the stiff form of the warrior for whom she was chosen. "My lord, please.

You see how he looks at me."

"He will not harm you, child. He is honor bound, like you." Dahru made certain the young warrior heard as well.

After a moment, Elenya nodded. She looked up at the stars, sucking in a then slowly exhaled breath before turning toward Tahruk. Head bowed, she followed, not bothering to fight the tears. Her dreams were shattered, the broken pieces washing away with each teardrop that fell onto the hand that held hers. Honor would have her pay for the sins of her ancestors.

She had been chosen to dance for a lifetime in the arms of her enemy.

At the request of readers, *Dance With The Enemy* has been expanded into a full-length novel, now available at Amazon. For additional information, visit www.lindaboulanger.com.

Dreams Belong

The rocking of Mahryn's body registered urgency even before her mind processed that she was being awakened.

"Mahryn, please. You need to rise and make ready. Quickly, child. You have a visitor." The head mistress' voice, raised an octave higher than usual, conveyed her anguish. Three other women bustled through the door of the small room Mahryn was allowed to call her own, all carrying items she'd need to do as the head mistress had commanded. No time was being wasted in her preparation.

Finally awake, her curiosity piqued, Mahryn sat up in her narrow bed and asked the obvious question. "May I inquire as to the visitor's identity, my lady?"

Eyes narrowed to match the thin line of her lips, the older woman fisted her full hips and stared first at a blank spot on the tinted wall and then at Mahryn. "Lord Sharanis has requested your presence." Toe tapping an annoying rhythm, she continued, "I don't know what you have done, as he declined to discuss matters with me, but he seemed most vexed."

A frown wrinkling her brow, Mahryn wondered at the peculiar visit. Not that she was surprised or even unhappy, by the guest's identity – the younger Sharanis had asked for her company many times, rewarding her with added gifts and favors after each encounter. She smiled inwardly. He was not so bad to look upon either. She didn't mind so much when he held her, though she could not imagine why he'd be displeased...

"The elder Sharanis!" the head mistress snapped, almost seeming to read the young lady's thoughts.

"The elder?" Why would Redahn's brother want to meet with her? Eyes widening, she slowly shook her head. Oh no. No, no, no. She'd heard dissention ran deep between these brothers, knew firsthand the tint of bitterness that had stained Redahn's words when he'd mentioned Tahruk. Surely that man had not heard of his brother's fancy for her and set out to take her from him...

"I suggest you step to, my lady. Believe me, you do not want to keep that old bear waiting any longer than you have to. I've seen firsthand how contemptuous he can be," the corisan told her while holding up a dress of burgundy taffeta overlaid with a shell of flimsy ivory gossamer for the head mistress' approving nod.

The chatter ceased as Mahryn slipped out of bed. Voices were replaced by the sound of bustling about in preparation for her meeting with Sharanis. Mahryn sat quietly, her hands folded in her lap. She looked around the room wondering how her life had ever come to this. Certainly this was not what she'd expected when she'd joined the other Dremis maidens at Dorengar's Centrehead. She felt cheated of her station, of the identity that went along with who she was, how she should have been treated. She was never meant to be a Lady of the Courts. Yet there she was.

She contemplated what this meeting with Sharanis could mean. She supposed being chosen as mistress to one of the kingdom's finest warriors, whether he was the man she desired or not, was better than what she had. At least she would be provided with a home of her own, and her children would be raised with the knowledge they belonged to one man, instead of simply being one of the many Children of the Courts who would go on to serve as corisans or any number of better positions within the castle...

Her transformation complete, the ladies went their way with the head mistress barking orders for Mahryn to follow her. Arms crossed over her chest, she scanned her room one last time, rubbing her hands up and down to ward off the cold bite of an emptiness that went far beyond the sparseness of the space she was allowed to call her own. Her eyes fell on the cross medallion lying on the small table next to her bed. A gift from her grandmother, it served to remind her that a higher authority was in charge, that even in the most tumultuous storms of life, she must not allow the darkness to overshadow her because one small ray of hope could cause the clouds to break, the light chasing away the darkness.

Mahryn had always been a dreamer, filled with hope and belief that everything would turn out okay, always looking for that silver lining. Closing the door behind her, she hoped her grandmother was right.

The man stood with his back to the door studying one of the art pieces placed around the room to appease the temperament of lords awaiting the presence of requested ladies. Mahryn frowned, unsure of whose back she was looking upon. Surely this older gentleman was not the stately warrior Redahn and others had spoken of when discussing Tahruk, though there was something oddly familiar about him. She was puzzled, even more so when he didn't grace the announcement of her presence with so much as a nod of confirmation for several moments after the door closed leaving them alone. Given to bouts of uncertainty as it was, Mahryn felt her confidence falter, the ray of hope dimming. She stood just inside the door, as still as any of the marble statues scattered about.

The man must have thought so too, his eyes darting from her to one statue in particular and then back again when he finally turned to face her.

"You are Mahryn?" he asked foregoing any semblance of formal introduction.

"Ye, yes, my lord." Her voice faltered slightly. She quietly cleared her throat in nervous anticipation of answering additional questions from this unknown man. She attempted to maintain eye contact, though the intensity of his stare made her look away, casting a furtive glance at the painting over his right shoulder. Her face reddening when she realized it was

Goridano's *Faded Boundaries* depicting the scene of an older man seducing a much younger maiden. She glanced back to see mirth lighting his eyes, even if it didn't make it to the rest of his features. Unnerved, she turned away, garnering a snort from the older man.

"What my son sees in you I am not quite sure, though I would agree you are not hard to look upon. Still, I would have expected a more assertive woman, given his nature."

His words turned her back to him, though it was less their abrasive nature as it was their use in identifying who he was.

"Redahn is your son, my lord?"

"*Lord* Redahn is, yes." He quirked a brow at her improper addressing of his son.

"Beg pardon, my lord." She dropped a stiff curtsy from her position across the room before employing her own blunt manner. "Please, may I inquire as to your reason for wishing to see me?"

The older man snorted again. "Perhaps I judged you prematurely." He crossed the room in few steps, moved her away from the wall with a fingertip pressed against her nearly bare back, and walked around her, assessing her much as one might a piece of livestock. It was no wonder those boys of his acted as they did, and it was on the tip of her tongue to tell him so when he silenced her with a finger to her lips.

"Smooth your ruffled feathers, would you. I'd like to offer you a proposal."

Standing in the confines of the waiting room, his finger still against her mouth, her blue eyes locked with his steely grays, Mahryn felt as if the world around her stood still as they began to spin. A proposal? She willed him to speak.

"I would like you to accompany me to Zanak Drille."

Mahryn's raised brow gained another snort. It was fairly obvious he was not inviting her into the most elite household outside the castle for his own sake.

"My oldest son's chosen is heavy with her second child. Extended rest has been advised…"

"Perhaps you have been misinformed. I am not a corisan, my lord."

He was already shaking his head. "She doesn't require someone to tend her needs. Lady Sharanis believes she needs a companion of sorts. Someone closer to her own age who might sit with her, read with her, perhaps engage in needlework or…" he waved a hand about, "whatever it is you women do when you are together."

He turned away, seeming to study the closest art piece. His agitation showed in the set of his strong shoulders, fists clenched at his sides.

"Why me?" she asked after failing to come to terms with his offer and his state. It wasn't that it was such an unusual request even. More that she was being singled out for the position when there were any number of young maidens specifically trained for such.

Lord Sharanis turned to stare at her again, the set of his jaw leaving her fearful he might recant his offer. Heaven knew, no matter the reason, it was a far cry better than finding herself on her back beneath different men at their discretion, and forced to act as if it was an honor to do so. She was fortunate that, presently, Redahn… *Lord* Redahn had been her only lover.

"I would be honored to accept your proposal, my lord," she told him with a low curtsy.

"Good. Now would you please gather your belongings so we may be on our way?"

His impertinence got the better of her and she answered him with her own question. "Would it not be fitting for you to address me as my lady, my lord? Perhaps you are not aware my father is Lord Tedran…" She let the name hang in the air.

He turned to her, eyes narrowed. "The King's second?" He shook his head. "No, *my lady*. He doesn't speak of having children beyond Hahna, his deceased daughter. Nor do you hail by his name. Perhaps you are mistaken."

Mahryn laughed a bit sadly, her chin going down to her chest before she spoke again, the silence punctuated by an unbidden sigh. "The use of his name was deemed unsafe. I do not believe he ever saw any of us beyond my sister anyway." Her eyes were wistful when she again looked up. "But I am, indeed, his daughter. You have but to look at my eyes if you need to be convinced."

The elder Sharanis did just that, bending close, turning her face toward the light with a finger beneath her chin. Surprise flickered in his own eyes as he recognized the faint flecks of gold within the blue, known so prominently to belong to the man heralded as the Kings closest confidant.

"Are you ill-gotten then?"

Mahryn's lower jaw dropped at the question of her legitimacy. She clamped it back shut to glare at him with thinned lips. Seconds ticked by before she answered. "I am *not*! I am Tedran's second daughter. His oldest, my full sister..." her voice broke slightly and resumed with only the touch of a tremor. "Hahna was marked, my lord. She was the chosen. Her death did not change that. It is a shadowed existence for those not first in line, regardless."

The older warrior studied her, his expression giving away nothing of what he might be thinking or feeling. With a curt nod, he turned and opened the door for her.

"I shall remain here while you gather your belongings," he told her. "Make haste, child. I grow impatient."

Mahryn left him to return to her room thinking she was quite sure his lack of patience began long before he came to visit her. She also wondered at the timing of his visit and the need to take her away during the darkness of the night. She could only hope it would all come together and make sense.

There it was again. Hope. The one thing she'd been able to rely on through her whole life. She lifted the heavy metal cross from the bedside table and slipped it over her head. She seldom wore it. Its size alone made it impractical most of the time and Mahryn had found she more enjoyed laying it about where she could see it. It brought her a sense of comfort and peace, much as the woman who'd given it to her.

"Never stop believing, Mahryn," her grandmother had told her as she sat beside the old woman's deathbed. "Dreams belong to those who can believe."

"I hope you are right, Grandmamma," she whispered before lifting her bag and walking through the door that would take her into the next phase of her young life. Suddenly, everything seemed brighter to her, even surrounded by the darkness of the night.

 Temptation's Whisper

She swung down from the tree, separating rider from horse with the contact of feet to chest as she fell. Christiana was tired of running and the only defense she could fathom was to take out her pursuer. The impact knocked her back, the horse's hooves barely missing her left hand before she could roll away and jump to the safety of her own two feet.

"Steady fella," she urged, grabbing the stallion's reins and instinctively cooing to the startled animal. His nostrils continued to flare, his head bucking, though he did not pull away. Slowly he steadied his prance, nuzzling the palm of the hand held toward him. "There you go. Now, you just hang tight while I check on your master." The rider had not moved from his prone position on the ground. Christiana pushed several errant strands of her dark hair behind her ear and bit at her lower lip, concern burning in her amber eyes. She strained, listening now that the horse had quieted. She heard no others close by within the forest. No one had bothered to attempt the densely grown trail up the hillside besides herself and this seemingly unshakeable man. It hadn't taken her long to realize the tree was her only hope.

Now, as she inched closer to him, she wasn't sure

whether she hoped he was dead or merely unconscious. She kicked at his booted foot with the tip of her toe. He didn't move. With slow, deliberate steps she worked her way to his side. The moment of truth was upon her. If he was faking, he would have her in a matter of seconds. At his size, his strength would quickly outmatch hers, whether he was hurt or not. With reflexes sharpened by the life she lived within the forest, Christiana's hand shot out and seized the hilt of his sword, unsheathing the metal blade with a force that knocked her backwards a good four or five steps before she regained her balance. Her heart pounded within her chest as she looked from the sword to the still man.

"Use the sword against him!" Temptation whispered.

Christiana knew it would take but one blow from the powerful, sharp-edged sword to sever his neck from his body. She'd be done with him and her safety would be assured, at least for another day. But murder… Survival was her nature, not murder. If he was not dead already, she could not bring herself to make it so. Head and hands both shaking, she looked back to the weapon, a groan ripping from her throat as she sank to her knees. Dear God, regardless of the outcome, she had already sealed her fate. She was holding the sword of the King.

Scrambling to his side, she wedged her feet beneath him and used her own body as a lever to roll him over. Yes, it was definitely the King, Lord Garrick Findlay Travensworth.

"Please don't be dead," she whispered, her fingers

trembling against his neck in an attempt to feel signs of life. If she was caught, wounding him would be bad enough. But if he was dead... There would be no hope. They would hunt her and her people, and the brutality of their executions... The thought made her shudder. Her mind clogged with fear and sudden uncertainty. She had to think of what she must do next.

Amber eyes darting around, she didn't notice the flinching of the King's hand, though she definitely heard his moan. That single sound pulled her from her moment of mental paralysis. He wasn't dead! But she had to do something, and quickly, before he regained full consciousness.

She jumped up, poised to run, then stopped. Dark red lips curved upward as the brave girl who had dared the hillside path and climbed the tree returned to her familiar self. *She* had the King! And the King would help her get her people back, unharmed. She would strike a bargain - their Lord for the freedom of her people. Complete freedom.

Careful, purposed steps returned her to his side where she dropped down and ran her hands along his body; something she should have done earlier. Relieving him of the dagger sheathed inside the sleeve of his tunic, she ran a hand around the top of his boot before removing the twin tucked within. Foolish oversight, she thought. Something she could not afford from here forward. Not if her forming plan was to succeed.

Biting at her lower lip, she carefully twisted the ring from his left hand and studied the emblem that should have created the King's Seal. Dark brows furrowed. It was incomplete from the seal on the intercepted correspondence that had led her people to this place today. Christiana had been the one chosen to carefully remove the wax marking from the letter, knowing that any flaw in the emblem replica would alert its recipients that confidentiality had been breached. The fact that the shipment of fine jewels had accompanied the King's bride-to-be through the forest that day was certain evidence that she had succeeded in its removal and return to the letter.

But this ring did not complete the seal.

"Without it, you have nothing." She heard the whisper again.

The urge to retreat welled once more, though it was quickly tamped down by another thought. She placed her palm against his chest and smiled. There. It had to be, she thought, reaching inside and yanking free from his neck the chain she had felt earlier. Without pause, she slipped the misshaped oval onto the outer edge of the ring. A perfect fit completing the design with subtle but necessary details; details she would not have recognized had she not been forced to learn because of the seal. She tipped her face to the heavens and offered a whispered thank you. Victory swirled around her, though she knew she must take care not to let it slip from her grasp as it had so many times from the hands of her ancestors. But *they* had never had the King, she though, turning her attention back to the man who had begun to stir at last.

"You!" His eyes fixed on her though his focus

seemed to continue to swim behind the dark blue depths. He carefully lifted his hand to his chest. "You've broken my ribs, wretch!"

Christiana laughed at him. "Nay, my lord. Were they broken, your breathing would be greatly labored. Bruised, perhaps. Broken? No." She stood just beyond his grasp, her hands on her hips as she stared down at him. The tales were correct. He was more handsome than a man had a right to be. "I'm sure you received far worse on the jousting fields in your day."

He stared at her, assessed her. She knew he was contemplating his surrounding and his ability to make a break to freedom.

"You might reconsider." Her tone was bolder than she felt. "I have your horse... and your seal." She held up the ring and watched him, knowingly. As expected, he felt his chest. "Looking for this?" She lifted the chained medallion and laughed at his surprise before slipping it down the front of her man tunic. She could feel it nestled safely inside her loosely laced corset. "Yes. I hold the key to your kingdom, my lord."

His face, as he watched her, twisted with an odd mixture of heightened interest and... admiration?

"And what will you do with your ill-begotten power?" Dark brows quirked at her, his eyes never leaving her face as he labored to push himself into a sitting position.

"Strike a bargain." A moment of confusion followed her words as she stepped back, wanting to distance herself from the rising King. She had not expected him to move so quickly.

It took him only three long strides to close the distance between them. He laughed as his hands went around her neck. Though frightened, Christiana did not cry out. She refused to give him the satisfaction. Her chest rose and fell as she stared up at him. He was a good foot taller than her. She swallowed hard knowing the thumbs pressed against her throat felt her every movement. She was desperately aware of him, his breath warm on her face, his body firm against hers.

Helpless to move, she watched his eyes dance over her face, stopping to gaze at her lips before those dark pools flicked back up. She was sure Temptation's whisper called to him from their amber depths.

"My lord." She tried to sound disdained, though achieved little more than a hoarse whisper.

His fingers snaked back into her dark curls as he closed the distance between them, his lips covering hers.

Christiana remembered the dagger, his dagger, slipped inside her own boot now. When he lowered her to the ground, as he surely would, she could retrieve it. But then…all hope would be gone.

Did hope remain? She wondered…

Two Kisses

By
Pat Sipperly & Linda Boulanger

All her life there'd been only two men she wished she'd kissed and didn't. Only two! TWO. Now we're not talking about a simple peck on the cheek or a faint brushing of the lips. No sir! She'd wanted them to be all out, set your watch, settle in for the count, write home to your best girlfriend, passion-filled kisses. Oh how many years now had she dreamed of these kisses? She'd tormented herself for not seizing the moment in each case.

Well, Mr. Opportunity was knocking on her door and each of these men had presented themselves back into her life. Both of them! Rachel smiled. How often did a girl get the chance to recapture a lost dream? Kind of like roping a rainbow. Oh the thoughts made her feel dizzy and slightly twitterpated.

She'd seen Kurt not too many years before. What had it been? Two? Maybe three. Either way, he'd looked mighty fine for a forty something, middle-aged man. Mighty fine indeed. But life had been different two, three years ago. She'd been madly in love with Jack. Kissing an old crush had been far from the front of her mind.

Now don't misunderstand. Rachel still loved Jack. In fact, he'd asked her to marry him. She'd agreed but had coaxed him into convincing her they should push the date a little ways down the road. She did love him. She did! He was nice looking, took care of himself, and he'd be a great provider and all. He even got along well with both of her grown children. But the sense of excitement at being together had waned somewhat. Okay, quite a bit. And now...she'd given her cell number to a mutual friend who had given it to Kurt and he'd called her for lunch. Lunch! With Kurt!!! One of her two missed opportunities. Lunch tomorrow...

Rachel shook her head and checked her emails. There it was...the confirmation for the thirty year reunion. Something else was there too. An email from Doug. Yep! The other guy she'd dreamed of for so very many years. They'd ran across each other quite by accident on the reunion pages and he still looked pretty darn good from his pictures anyway. Several emails confirmed them into the mutual admiration club and arrangements were made to meet a day earlier than the reunion. Oh yes! Rachel touched her flushed cheeks and laughed like a silly school girl. She felt as giddy as a seventeen year old in young love.

The next day found her trying on outfit after outfit until she found the one that portrayed the perfect look. Hands on hips, she turned this way and that looking at her image. Now she looked good for 48! She was still trim. Her hair was dark with just the right highlights. Eyes were still bright. And the outfit made her look...well, just a little bit like a hottie. Not a tramp! Just desirable. She was ready. With a smack of her painted lips she sauntered out of the house to meet Kurt. Today was THE day! She was determined to make it happen.

They were to meet at McDaniel's Bar & Grill. She'd made the reservations, requested the perfect table. In her mind she'd played through the scene over and over. They'd be seated adjacently, their chairs both too close to the corner. They'd chat, she'd flirt unabashedly and, by the end of the meal, he'd kiss her. She felt all tingly as she drove.

The young lady at the front knew her. She nodded when Rachel said she could seat herself. As she walked toward the requested table, a surge of irritation rose up. Someone else had sat down there! Some pudgy older man with thinning, bristly gray hair and a wrinkled face had dared to interfere with her dream. Her heart sank as he looked up at her and smiled. She'd have known those blue eyes anywhere; those blue eyes that washed over her with unchecked appreciation.

"Kurt!" she said with faux-enthusiasm. "How nice to see...how nice of you to have agreed to meet me for lunch." She quickly slipped on the little sweater she'd draped over her arm just in case it was too cold.

It was a nice lunch after all. Great catching up. They'd always been comfortable with each other. As he kissed her cheek in the parking lot, Rachel guessed it would always be that way.

In all her life there was only one man Rachel Dunbar wished she'd kissed but hadn't. One Douglas Taylor. Doug, as all his friends called him. He'd been such a sweet guy in High School. Always the perfect gentleman, even when they'd huddled close together against the cold on the bus with the broken window coming home after a football game. The cheerleader and the quarterback. It would have been so perfect. Yet neither of them pursued it. And now, thirty years later to find out both had harbored feelings for one another.

The plane landed and she knew he'd be there to meet her even though she'd told him she could get her own car. Her heart beat wildly, hopeful his photos hadn't lied.

She breathed a sigh of relief as she stepped through the gate and caught sight of him. Now Doug Taylor looked good with a capital G-O-O-D for a 48 year old man. Dang! Wow! No disappointment there.

"Rachie!" He grabbed her up and swung her around. She giggled, oblivious to the people who stared. "You look great, girlie."

"Well!" She stepped back and surveyed him openly. "you weren't lying when you said you'd taken care of yourself." They walked from the airport arm in arm.

"Watch out rainbow," Rachel thought, "I'm getting out my rope."

By the end of the next day Rachel wondered what she had gotten herself into. Doug had indeed taken care of himself and was truly the center of his own universe. Every conversation came back to him. He was extremely opinionated and well...yawn, boring. Doug, blah blah. Doug, bleh bleh bleck. Why had she not seen this in the emails?

The weekend could not pass quickly enough for her. Although she did enjoy seeing Jilly, Susan, Marjorie and the others again. She was happy to say she was still the best looking of the squad. But she was ecstatic when Doug dropped her at the airport. She departed with but a little kiss on the forehead.

Jack met her at the door of her townhouse with a lovely, hand-tied bouquet of flowers. She could smell a delicious meal in the makings. Dropping her bags she threw herself into him, nearly crushing the flowers. Carelessly he tossed them on the side table and wrapped her in his arms. His hands ran up her spine and into her hair, pulling her head back with gentle ease. With a smile, he lowered his lips to meet hers.

Breathless, Rachel looked up at Jack with dreamy admiration and desire. In all her life there was not a man she wanted to be kissed by more than Jack Reed. In fact, there had never been a man she'd wanted to kiss and didn't.

Sidenote from Linda: Two Kisses is one of my favorite stories. It began with an idea I had because, you see, there are only two guys in my life that I wish I'd kissed and didn't! I won't. Both are now dear friends -- and they have no idea they're "the ones" that inspired this fun little story.

The story began a bit more serious in nature, although by the time I sent the original to my co-writer, Pat Sipperly, it had evolved. He took it and further added his own special blend of humor and, I must say, I am so pleased with this story. You can find it in our co-written collection titled *Time Out On A Roller Coaster*.

Enjoy Novellas?
Check out Linda Boulanger's

Arms of an Angel

Being wealthy and beautiful doesn't promise an automatic ticket for happiness. Sometimes you need the angelic touch of someone who needs you as much as you need him… Sometimes it's hard to tell where one set of wings ends and the other begins.

Claire is alluring, sensual – called an angel by some, though the woman she's become is anything but celestial. Her heart is filled with pain so deeply embedded she doesn't want to live any longer…until fate puts her into the hands of the most virtuous man she's ever met; a man who needs someone like Claire to help him piece together the shattered bits of his own life.

Enjoy an excerpt…

Excerpt from
Arms of an Angel
©2011 Linda Boulanger

"You want to come up? We can have that coffee we never ordered…" They were stopped in front of the building waiting for a clearing to turn into the circle drive where the doorman waited. Their eyes locked and a bucket of emotions passed between them.

He reached over and touched her cheek. "I want to, but I won't. Besides, I have a brunch date at my parent's farm in Morgan's Falls. It's late and I'll have to get up early to make it on time."

"Oh." Claire nodded, the corners of her lips turning down. "A decent reason I suppose." She chuckled. "I've never been turned down for parents."

They smiled at one another as he pulled in and the doorman approached. "Another time perhaps?"

Claire gave a noncommittal half shrug. "Perhaps." She was silent for a moment, signaling the doorman to wait. "Thank you for an enjoyable evening, Garrett. I'm pleased our paths crossed." She started to reach for the door and he grasped her arm. She looked at his hand then at him.

"I have this overwhelming feeling that I'll never see you again once you get out." His brows were drawn down, his face concerned.

Claire was sure he could hear the loud thud of her heart. She felt the need to throw him off.

"Let me have your phone." She held out her hand and he produced it with out question. She stared at it for a moment then keyed in her number. "There." She handed it back.

"Thank you." He smiled, rubbing the phone between his fingers as if it was her hand. "We'll have that coffee… and sooner than you think.

"Would we have had coffee, Dr. O'Bryan?" she asked, kissing his cheek and bolting from the car before he had time to recover.

When she waved and smiled mischievously from the lobby doorway he shook his head and laughed. The thought of her would not easily be shaken, he was sure of that.

"You're home early, Ms. Orion," Garrett heard the doorman saying to her as he pushed the button that rolled down the window. "And alone! You ruffled somebody's feathers again, girl?"

Claire started to respond but was cut off by Garrett's voice calling her name. She turned toward him and he was struck momentarily silent by her beauty. Uncertain of his intent, she walked back to the car and looked through the open window.

"Change your mind?" she teased. "No, I suppose Morgan's Falls still has you bound. What then?"

"Sunday brunch? 10:00ish? And we'll have that coffee then. Scouts honor." He held up two fingers.

"Wouldn't you know. Friday night and I get stuck with a parent whipped boy scout." She laughed, letting him know she was still teasing. "Make it 10:30 and I'll accept with expectation."

Garrett nodded. "Claire," he called as she began to back away. "You are a woman of your word, right?" When she didn't respond he added, "You seem as though you would be."

Claire breathed in and held it for a moment as she

looked into the distance. The night had not gone as she'd planned. Now she was being asked for her word. Yes, she was a woman of her word…most of the time, and especially when pressed. Why was he asking? Did he inherently know? If she said yes, under the circumstances, was she bound by her word? Yes, she supposed she was. At last she nodded. "My yes is yes. I'll be waiting and watching. 10:30 sharp on Sunday morning."

Garrett smiled. "Thank you."

"You may change your mind. You don't really know me." She pushed away from the car with a laugh.

He shook his head. No, he didn't know her at all. He'd lived enough of life, however, to believe their paths must have crossed that evening for a definite reason. He wondered if he'd ever find out why.

"You losin' your touch, Miss?" Garrett heard the doorman teasing her again.

"Nah, Charlie. I got lucky in a different way tonight." She elbowed the older gentleman. "I found me an angel. What was his name? Clarence maybe? Oh listen… I think I hear a bell ringing."

He heard the doorman chuckle as Claire disappeared behind the heavy wood and beveled glass doors of the grand building.

"Not an angel with these thoughts!" he whispered as he drove away.

About Linda Boulanger

Linda Boulanger is a happily-ever-after author, wife, and mother of four. She has an eclectic mix of published books, numerous story singles and short stories in a few group anthologies, plus several more novels slated for release this year and next.

Along with being an author, she designs book covers for herself and others through Tell~Tale Book Covers and TreasureLine Designs, all from her desk just north of Tulsa, Oklahoma.

Other place to find Linda:

Website: http://www.LindaBoulanger.com

Blog: http://writersshelflife.blogspot.com/

FaceBook:
https://www.facebook.com/TheShelfLifeOfLindaBoulanger

Email: lindaboulangerauthor@gmail.com

Linda's Writing...

Novels/Novellas
Dance With the Enemy
Arms of an Angel

Anthologies
Time Out on a Roller Coaster
Becoming…
Whispered Beginnings
Echoed Heartbeats

Color Illustrated Children's Book
How Sadie Learned to S.M.I.L.E.

Short Story Trios and Singles (Kindle)
Up To Bat / Center Stage / Best Friend Rules
Face of an Angel / Life Changes / Talk With Me
Temptation's Whisper
Secret Shame

Coming Soon
Dance Beyond the Shadows
The Perfect Gift
Dance to Temptation's Whisper
Marriage of Necessity
Selling Ellie